A MOMENT OF WEAKNESS

a Boston Alibi novel

BROOKLYN SKYE

Entangled Publishing, LLC
2614 South Timberline Road
Suite 109
Fort Collins, CO 80525
Visit our website at www.entangledpublishing.com.

Brazen is an imprint of Entangled Publishing, LLC. For more
information on our titles, visit www.brazenbooks.com.

Edited by Heather Howland
Cover design by Heather Howland
Cover art from Shutterstock

Manufactured in the United States of America

First Edition October 2015

**ENTANGLED
BRAZEN**

For Ryan, always.

Chapter One

Micah Crane's fist collided with the guy's face for what he hoped was the last time. He'd known the shithead would fight back—they always did—but this guy was huge, at least two-seventy-five to Micah's two-twenty.

"Who are you with again?" the guy gasped, wiping the bead of blood from his split lip.

Micah laughed, the sound echoing down the length of the dark alley. "You have debts with *more* than one associate?" He shook out his hand, the deep ache in his knuckles dulling. "Either you're really fucking stupid or a walking death wish." Or both. And Micah didn't care. While roughing guys up wasn't exactly a *chosen* profession, the guys he was paid to "handle" for Russo were all hoods who needed to have the shit beat out of them anyway.

The guy sat up and coughed. "I—"

"Shut your mouth," he said with a raise of his hand. Don't ask, don't tell. A strict policy he held when dealing with these douchebags. Micah didn't want to know what they owed, or why. It made him feel like less of an asshole when going home to his daughter every night.

Eyes not leaving the guy, he bent to retrieve his bat, thankful he hadn't had to use it. Fists first, but in this business, protection was necessary.

"Settle up with Russo by the end of tomorrow," he said, back-stepping toward the mouth of the alley. "Or you can deal with the guy who comes after me. And he likes to enter his get-togethers carrying a shovel, if you know what I mean."

It was only a short drive to the Central Burying Ground but plenty of time for Micah's heart to jump into overtime. Meeting with Russo was his least favorite part of the job, but the associate for the well-known organized crime family insisted on doing things face to face. And one thing his father had taught him… *Do what they say, stay on their side, and all will be well in your wallet.*

He chuckled to himself. Yeah, the pay was damn good all right. Enough to cover what The Alibi—the bar he co-owned with his best friend—didn't. Shaelynn deserved the best school in Boston, especially now that she was entering first grade.

He parked in the shadows and stole past the eerie span of rickety gravesites—artists, poets, composers…people who'd made a difference, been important; people who were nothing like him—and stopped at the plaque of The Great Elm. Uneven and crumbling at the edges, the marker sat where a giant tree, once a point of fortification and used in hangings, had stood. *Fitting*, he couldn't help but think every time he set foot near it.

Russo emerged from the surrounding trees, his arms held wide. "How long did it take this time? Wait, let me guess. Five hits? Six?" He smiled, his teeth gleaming in the moonlight. "Asshole was huge, huh?"

Huge enough to ask for a heftier fee, yes, but he wouldn't dare. He nodded to Russo with his chin. "Can we make this quick? I've got to get back to work." Rather, back to Shaelynn. But he'd never talk to this man—or any of the associates—about his daughter. Regardless, Russo was a member of the most powerful crime family in the state. Of *course* he knew about her. Micah had seen the man in his bar a few times. Watched him order one drink, make eye contact with him, and then leave with a sleazy grin on his even sleazier mouth. An acknowledgement on Russo's part that he could hold everything Micah had over his head if Micah didn't produce.

He'd never let this man touch his daughter.

Russo exposed a wad of bills from his jacket pocket and handed it to Micah. "When can I expect my money?"

"He'll pay by the end of tomorrow." And he knew the thug in the alley would. They always did after a visit from him. It was why he'd had a continuous stream of jobs from Anthony Russo, whether he wanted them or not.

A fter a quick stop at the gas station to clean up, Micah entered The Alibi. A few of his regulars sat along the bar, chatting and guffawing with the bar's longtime bartender Trey—a thirty-something ginger with a laugh that could draw in the ladies. A pair of younger-looking guys—closer to his little sister's age than his—stood belly up to the bar, a beer in each of their hands. Micah had never seen them before.

No ladies tonight either, he noticed on his way to the back room he and Ryan used as their office. With the dilapidated sign hanging out front and sketchy projects surrounding their neighborhood block, it took a severe case of martini goggles for Boston's women to make their way into his small, ramshackle bar, which usually didn't happen until well past midnight.

In his office, he tucked the wad of cash from Russo into the safe hidden in the file cabinet and started to work on payroll. The bar didn't revenue enough to pay for a bookkeeper, and this was his least favorite part of the job. Sitting behind a desk had never been his thing. *Maybe if it was, Shae would have a better life.*

At the thought of his daughter, the back door swung open and she skipped in and jumped onto his lap. "Daddy!" Six years old and still wanting to sit on his lap—he hoped she'd never stop.

Kissing her temple, he ran his hand down her wavy blonde hair. "Hi, princess. How was your day?"

"The best! Uncle Ryan took me to get ice cream. For dinner! Chocolate with Oreos."

"Your favorite," Micah said to her with a discreet what-the-fuck glance at his partner.

Ryan shrugged and jerked the black beanie off his head, his normally slicked-back hair looking more like a dirty mop. "You told me to keep her happy."

He did. He also hadn't had a choice when Russo texted him last minute with an assignment.

"We went to watch chickens wrestle too," Shae said with a grin, stealing his pen to draw a heart on the back of his hand. "I didn't like that, though. They were being mean to each other."

Micah scowled at Ryan. "You took her to a cockfight? How is that appropriate for a six-year-old?"

"Hey," Ryan spouted, roughly combing his fingers through his thick beard, "You weren't the only one who had sh— I mean crap to get done. Jackson needed to meet about the Bud account. I had no choice."

Shae leaned in and, with a giggle, whispered into Micah's ear, "*Shit*, Daddy. He was going to say 'shit.'"

"I know, baby girl." Micah nuzzled her close. Jesus, his little girl wasn't a baby he could entertain in an Exersaucer in the back room anymore. Every day, she was growing more perceptive, more aware of the world and the life he'd spent building for her. A life, he thought as he scanned the dingy room, that wasn't fit for the princess she was. He kissed her head again. "But you're better than crazy Uncle Ryan, so I don't want you saying it."

The words came out, but the conviction in them was missing. Ryan glanced at him, his eyes seeming to ask exactly what Micah was thinking. Would Shae really grow up to be better than them if he continued to drag her to The Alibi? Drag her into a life no better than the one he was raised in?

Chapter Two

Laurel Harris's eyes flickered back and forth between the red-haired director sitting across the desk from her and the notes she scrawled every time Laurel answered one of her questions.

What is your highest level of education completed?

Do you have your teaching certification?

All applicants require a background check. Would this be a problem?

Being the city's most prestigious daycare, Ivy League Childcare Center was more ostentatious than the others she'd interviewed at, looking more like a fancy hotel than a place for kids. No matter. It was a job—something she desperately needed.

Laurel toyed with the scratchy material of her skirt and smiled. These questions she'd answered on the application, and if the woman stuck to them, she'd have no trouble finishing out this interview.

A strand of hair drifted loose from the woman's bun and stuck to her lips as she tilted her head and asked, "How many years of experience do you have teaching children?"

Laurel shifted her shoulders back. "I don't have any years teaching yet. I grew up babysitting all the kids in my neighborhood and helping my parents, who are both teachers, in their classrooms. I've already been hired with the school district for the fall, so I'm really just looking for something to keep me busy throughout the summer."

Or to pay her rent check.

Eat three meals a day like normal people who have jobs.

Save for school supplies for her new classroom.

She pinched her lips into a smile.

"Just the summer?" the woman asked, stilling her pen along the paper. Beneath the desk, the woman's legs uncrossed, and something about that movement sent Laurel's heart skittering up toward her necklace. Would the little arrow charm start to bounce? Would the woman see it?

The director set the pen down. "Here at Ivy League, we place a high amount of importance on keeping our center family oriented. In doing so, we create bonds with children and parents that last long past when they leave our program. Part of that process is finding teachers who desire long-term employment, not just a summer job." She stood. "Thank you for your time." Her hand shot out, opened and ready to shake.

Wait. She was ending the interview already?

Laurel pried herself from the chair, the words *way to ruin the interview* floating through her head.

"We'll be in touch with you once we make our decision," the woman added as she escorted Laurel to the door then shut it behind her. Laurel had been on enough interviews to know that the blunt tone of the woman's voice meant she wouldn't be calling.

She closed her eyes and stole a breath. Ivy League was the last on her very short list of hiring daycares. The breath released. How would she pay her rent through the summer?

Driving home, Laurel scanned the storefronts—coffee shops, clothing boutiques, jewelry, shoes... Maybe she'd apply at some of those. Or all of them. Yes, definitely all of them.

A sudden burst of energy struck her as she parked in front of the old house she'd been renting a room from, a mental list of businesses she'd submit applications to running through her head. She didn't have a choice. Her parents had some money but were on tight budgets of their own, which didn't allow enough to loan her for her summer rent.

Up the cracked walkway, her landlord Ms. Hastings emerged from the front door. The woman looked as old as the house, just as weathered too. The type that knew age was stealing her brain and didn't like it one bit. Laurel waved with a forced smile then ducked her head, praying there'd be no mention of the two-day-late rent notice currently sitting on her kitchen counter. She only had half the amount so far.

Ms. Hastings knitted her brows together in a *your rent is due, young lady* scolding sort of look but thankfully didn't say it.

Inside her tiny room, she settled at the makeshift desk in front of her computer, ready to spend the rest of the evening with a deluge of online applications. She could do this.

She *had* to do this.

A few hours later, a yellow, rubber...*what would I even*

call that? appeared in front of her face.

"It's called The Tickler," her best friend April supplied, jiggling the...*thing*. It looked like a colorful pig's tail with a nub on each end.

"A what?" Laurel rolled back her shoulders and creaked her neck to the side. How many applications had she just filled out?

Her roommate fingernailed a tiny switch, and it started vibrating.

"Oh my god," Laurel said, pushing it away. "Why are you showing this to me? I don't need to know what you do while I'm sleeping." She pointed to the wall where a few of her pictures hung. "Do you know how thin this house's walls are?" It had been a joke when the two of them had rented side-by-side rooms from Ms. Hastings. A snicker and smirk from April, knowing the chances of hearing Laurel with a man was slim.

"It's not for me," April said. "I got it for you. You know, since you don't *ever* let a man do the job for you." She held up the contraption. "The package says it's a rabbit vibe, a clitoral massager, a cock ring, and a G-spot stimulator all in one." Her bright red lips stretched into a smile as she plopped it into Laurel's lap, still pulsating. "You can thank me later."

"I'll thank you *never*. I'm not using that." Sure, her roommate was right—she didn't bring men home. Nor did she go home with them. One night of pleasure then a week of hoping he would call wasn't all that appealing now that she'd graduated college and was trying to make something of herself.

April leaned in, eyeing the classifieds list on the

computer. "How'd the interview go?"

"They were looking for long-term employees, not people only for the summer." She sat back in her chair and sighed. "Finding a summer job has been way harder than I expected."

April perched at the edge of the desk and tapped her long acrylic fingernails against it, screwing up her face at the same time. "Kids... I can't believe you want to voluntarily insert yourself into a room of them."

Laurel shrugged. "What could be scarier than kids?"

"Slimy, snotty kids."

They both laughed. Okay, maybe she was right there. But both her parents were elementary school teachers, and ever since first grade, when her teacher told her to walk around the classroom and show every student how awful her work was, Laurel had known becoming a teacher who didn't create a negative environment for kids was what she wanted to do. She'd heard stories from her parents about the nation being so focused on test results and high scores that true teaching was very quickly being replaced with teaching to the test. Pressure like that was sure to increase stress among teachers, and therefore students, and Laurel knew deep in her heart that situations like that would only leave kids with a bitter taste in their mouths regarding school. Then what kind of adults would they grow into? What kind of generation would follow hers?

"I have an idea," April said, sitting taller. Her thin, floral blouse stretched against her bony shoulders. "Or a temporary one that might get you through the next few months. My big brother has a daughter and could really use some help with her. Why don't I talk to him? He could probably take you on for the summer."

Already, Laurel was shaking her head. "I'm looking for an actual job, Ape, not a babysitting gig. We're not seventeen."

"She needs a role model too."

"So why don't you do it? You *are* her aunt."

"Uh, no," April said, her nose scrunched. "The girl is cute, and I love her to death, but there's no way I could spend my afternoons with peanut butter and washable markers." She gave Laurel a *Have you seen me?* kind of look, and Laurel laughed. Yeah, the image of her over-the-top, skincare-selling friend acting motherly *was* amusing. Then April sprang to her feet and ran out of the room, heels tapping along the wooden hallway to her room. Over her shoulder, she sang out, "I'm calling him!"

The Alibi. Was her best friend crazy? Meeting for a job interview at a *bar*? And a decrepit one at that?

Laurel straightened her skirt, adjusted the silky white blouse she'd borrowed from April, and yanked open the bar's bright-orange door. Hot, alcohol-stenched air burned her nose as she stepped across the grime-encrusted floor to the bar extended along the back wall.

"What can I get you?" the bartender said, at the same time dunking a pint glass into a vat of soapy water.

"Actually…" Laurel cleared her throat and said, "I have a meeting with one of the owners. Micah Crane? His sister arranged for me to meet him here."

The bartender smiled, the blizzard of freckles on his

nose scrunching into a solid plane. "He had to run a quick errand. He'll be back in a minute." Then he pointed to a barstool. "Have a seat, and I'll get you something to drink. What'll it be?"

She glanced around the empty bar and then to her watch. Four o'clock. Certainly too early for a drink. Especially on this side of town, where she'd likely have to utilize her pepper spray once the sun went down. "A Shirley Temple, please." She said it with a smile, hoping he wouldn't see the way her body was strung tight. Sheesh, why was she so nervous? She didn't even want this job—was only there to meet Micah because she hadn't heard a single word from any of the businesses she'd applied to, and over the last two days, Ms. Hastings's stern looks had morphed into full-on scowls. But she needed money and was willing to take whatever work she could find.

The bartender poured the drink, topping it off with a few cherries, then continued to wash the stack of dirty glasses. He didn't talk to her, which she appreciated. She took a sip of the sweet fizziness. Then another. And just as she tipped the glass to her lips for a third time, the door opened and in walked a man. Huge, menacing, and…undeniably gorgeous with a mess of dark hair, stubble on his cheeks, and brown eyes that literally sparkled under the bar's fluorescent lighting.

Holy hell, so much brown has never looked so delicious.

"That's him," the bartender said, nodding his chin to the ominous figure crossing the room. The man's waist was slim, his shoulders broad, and Laurel's belly button tingled at the thought of what that would look like shirtless. Based on the size of his arms and the smoothness of his skin, the sight would definitely be worth seeing—

In a flash, the glass slipped off her bottom lip, and ice-cold liquid showered down the front of her shirt.

"Oh my gosh." She hopped off her seat. "I'm so sorry. I'll clean it up," she said to the bartender. "Let me just…" The front of her shirt, now pink, clung to her skin. *This would be your cue to leave, Laur. Before your potential new boss sees the mess you made in his bar and becomes the next person to politely say, "We'll be in touch."*

Her feet stuck to the floor. No, she wouldn't run out because of a small spill. Quickly she scanned the area, spotted the ladies' room, and booked it.

The bathroom was a box of a room, but it had a mirror and sink—two things necessary to salvaging this meeting. Standing in front of her reflection, Laurel assessed the damage. The pink liquid had soaked completely through the white material, suction cupping to and revealing her nude-colored bra beneath. Okay, so maybe there was no salvaging.

She called April. "You're done already?" her roommate asked when she picked up.

"Why didn't you tell me your brother is a scary sex god?" she whispered into the phone. Best friends were supposed to tell each other stuff like that, right?

"Of course he is. How could I be related to anything less?" April laughed. "Is that why you're interrupting my pedicure slash business meeting?"

Huh? That didn't even make sense. April had been working as a sales consultant for a high-end company called Luxury Skincare, something she proved to be really, really good at based on the way she showed up each week with new clothes, shoes, nail color…

In a rush, Laurel grabbed a handful of paper towels and tried to mop up the mess on her top. "Um, no," she said, awkwardly pinching the phone between her cheek and shoulder. "But I might've spilled Shirley Temple on your shirt. How do I get it out?"

Just then, a knock sounded on the bathroom door, and before Laurel could respond, Micah Crane barged in. Instinctively, she retreated a step back, an uncontrollable flush of heat rushing out from her chest. *Uh, hello?* Women's restroom. Huge, ridiculously gorgeous male taking up way too much space, running his eyes over the pink shirt plastered to her breasts. *The same color as my cheeks, I'm sure.* Just the thought intensified the temperature, spreading it over every inch of her body. "I have to go," she said into the phone, not waiting for April's response before hitting end and tucking the phone into her purse. Then she looked up to the stunning man, trying not to notice that up close—very, very close—his brown eyes were freckled with the color of citrine, then steadied herself with a hand on the cold sink. This off-kilter feeling he gave her... Was this what it was like being rammed by a truck? Attraction at first sight; didn't that only happen in movies?

Slowly she stuck out her other hand and forced a smile. "Um, hi. I'm here for the babysitting interview?"

*B*abysitting? Was April on crack?

In their phone call yesterday, his sister had said one of her roommates needed a job. As in a bartending job, or so he thought. But looking over this girl... What was she, like twenty-two? Innocent to a tee with big doe eyes and a trembling smile. No, she wouldn't be looking for a job on this side of town. Hell, why was she outside of Cambridge anyway? *A girl like her would get eaten alive out here.*

Micah narrowed his eyes. "What exactly did my sister tell you?"

"Um…" Her gaze flickered down to her soaked shirt. Micah's eyes followed, lingering for a moment on the outline of lace beneath the see-through material. "You have a daughter," she said, standing with an unnatural stillness. "And that you could use some help with her. Maybe it was a mistake. I can just go…"

He almost laughed. Help with Shae? Like hell he did; he'd been managing just fine alone.

Or was he? Keeping her here at the bar, entertaining her in the back office with a pad of paper and a multicolored pen while he put in hours and snuck off to fulfill Russo's requests… Was that the best way to raise his daughter?

It wasn't. That much was obvious. But bringing someone he didn't know into their lives—into their *home*—to keep Shae out of the bar didn't sit well, either.

The wet-shirted woman tugged at the material again then reached for her phone. "Maybe I should call April back?"

"No need," he said, closing his hands around her phone. He would be the first one to call her, to tell her off for setting him up like this. The girl—Laurel, was that what April had told him?—shrank away from his touch. "And, yeah, it was a mistake," he added. "I'm not looking for a nanny." Not willing to put Shae in danger by bringing an absolute stranger into his home no matter how innocent this girl looked or how well she knew his sister. If working for Russo taught him one thing, it was to trust no one.

He held open the door and stepped to the side, a hint to Laurel that it was time for her to go. This day had already been a clusterfuck, after Russo's cousin had been arrested for extorting thousands of dollars in protection payments from a video poker machine company. Not Micah's problem, only it was when Russo was pissed and requesting deadlines that were practically unfeasible.

Micah didn't have time for any of this.

"Daddy?" Shae suddenly said from the end of the hallway, standing just outside the office door. "Can we go home yet? I'm bored."

Micah hustled to her and crouched down to her level, swiping his hand over her head. He'd had her here for more than three hours, keeping her busy with made-up filing tasks and games on his phone, but— "I still have some work to do, baby girl. It'll be a little longer. How about you go help Trey wash the glasses?" Micah lifted his daughter's hand and kissed it. "And tell him I said you can have as many cherries as you want."

Shae shook her head and puffed out her bottom lip. "I just want to go home," she said, and that fucking melted his heart. In a line down the middle of his core, it stung as if he was being ripped in half. Every day that passed, it was becoming clearer and clearer; he needed to work something else out.

But not a nanny. Not anyone he didn't know.

Down the hall, he caught sight of Laurel standing in the bathroom doorway. *Why is she still here?* And why was she looking at him that way—like her insides were being pulled in two different directions too?

Laurel watched as Micah Crane tapped the little girl's nose with his finger and said, "I promise I'll do something with you later if you stay in the office for a few more minutes." Why was there a child—his daughter, evidently by the way she called him "Daddy"—hanging out in a bar? On this side of town? By herself, where anyone could mistake that door for the bathroom and find her?

Was anyone even watching her?

The girl peeked around him to Laurel with a crinkle in her brow. "You spilled on your shirt."

"I did," Laurel said, her chest aching at the thought that this small child—not more than five or six—was spending her time with intoxicated men and the stench of old alcohol.

"It's a pretty shirt. And I like it pink."

Laurel smiled down at Micah's daughter. "It belongs to your Aunt April. I'll tell her you said so."

Micah opened the door and nudged his daughter back in, then turned to Laurel, scrubbing a hand over his face. She wanted to run in there to get the girl and scream at Micah for allowing his daughter in a bar in the first place. And yet her body wanted to do something else entirely, like climb his huge, muscled body like a tree.

She shook off that last thought and suppressed the untimely giggle that accompanied it. Inappropriate thought about man she was sent to interview with? *Yeah, it may be time to test out The Tickler.*

Her eyes fell on the door, to the image of a little girl

sitting alone in that room. "You…" Laurel said, pausing to gather her words. "You bring your daughter to a bar? And let her hang out unsupervised in the back?" *Would Child Protective Services allow that?*

Micah shrugged. "We weren't busy today…" The words sounded innocent enough—a guy in a pinch for someone to watch his kid. But Laurel caught something more; a heaviness that probably meant he brought her here on eventful nights too.

She ground her teeth, her body tensing from her toes up to her ears. What kinds of things did this little girl see in a bar? What kinds of people talked to her?

"And if you were busy…?" The little girl's pinched face and pouty lips burned in Laurel's mind. She eased a step back, pointed to the closed door beside him, and lowered her voice so the girl wouldn't hear. "Drug dealers…drunk men…anyone looking for the restroom could stumble down the hall and find her. And you, occupied with whatever you do out there"—she waved her hand in the direction of the bar area—"would never know."

With lines of cords drawing up his thick neck, Micah shoved his hands into his pockets and started down the hall, away from the room his daughter was in. "I've got inventory to finish. Do you need me to show you the door?"

He was leaving his daughter. *Again.*

Laurel glanced up and down the dim corridor, the need to run in and comfort the little girl burning clear down to her fingertips. Was she scared to be in that room alone? And what about safety? Was there anything that could injure her if she got into it?

Without thinking, Laurel grabbed Micah's gigantic

forearm as he passed. Hard muscle tensed beneath the pads of her fingers. Huh. How did someone get such strong forearms?

Laurel shook her head. *You really need to stay focused!* She cleared her throat. "Your daughter's not safe in there," she said. "No child would be, regardless of how often she's been coming here."

He jerked his arm away from her and stepped closer, towering over her. Suddenly, it was like her heart had grown arms and was clawing its way up her chest and into the hollow of her throat. He was so big…and scary…and even more mouthwatering this close up, despite the yellowish bruise sitting like a puddle high on his cheek.

She pressed her backside into the bathroom door. His hands braced the wall on both sides of her head, caging her in like a trapped animal. *Breathe, Laurel.*

Warm breath brushed along her skin with the words, "I don't have a choice." His brown eyes narrowed, hard and piercing. "And I haven't since her mother left her on my doorstep then took off." His arms fell away, but his face remained planted in front of her, not blinking at all. "Now if you'll excuse me, I have work to finish." Slowly he backed away, the pressure lifting from her chest with every inch of space he created.

The girl didn't have a mother in her life, either? When April had mentioned her brother being a single dad, she had simply assumed he'd been married, had a kid, then gotten divorced. Not abandoned with a baby the mother didn't want.

The poor child.

Micah spun, his back now to her.

"Wait," Laurel blurted out, pushing off the door and stepping toward him. What if she could make this little girl's life better? Take her out of the bar and instead do something productive with her? "Let me help you. Please. A bar is no place for a child. I can watch her during the days you're working. Maybe take her to the park or work with her on skills she'll need for school? Reading? Math—"

"I don't need your help," he growled, clenching his hands into tight fists.

"Really?" A challenging tone laced the word. What would this little girl grow up like if he continued to raise her in a bar? "Because this right here, with a small child stuck in the back room of a bar while her father works, looks like you might."

Silence. Nothing. Why was he so opposed to someone helping him? Did he actually think he was doing a good job?

She took another step closer and softened her voice. "Listen, I'm a friend of your sister's, not some random person off the street. Not even a stranger you could hire through a nanny company. Plus, I'm a credentialed teacher. I've had background checks done on me—which I'm sure you could get a copy of if you wanted." She took a breath. What else could she say to get through to him? She gestured to the door. "All I see is a precious little girl who would be much better off if she were living a normal childhood."

At those last words, something in his tough expression changed. Tempered. She couldn't put her finger on exactly what had changed—maybe the deep divot drawn between his brows or the sharp angle of his mouth. He stood still for a moment, his eyes locked on the door behind her, and rubbed the back of his neck.

One breath, two. Why did he have to think twice about this?

Finally, his gaze found hers. "The background check. If I agree to this, I want access to it."

"Done."

"And no dates with your boyfriend while you have her."

The corners of Laurel's mouth pushed into her cheeks. What was she, seventeen and babysitting the neighbor kids? She shook her head. "Nothing to worry about there. I'm not seeing anybody."

Heat flushed through her with those words. He wasn't looking for permission to do anything, so why did it feel like he was suddenly devouring her with his eyes? Skimming down her knee-length skirt and over her simple black ballet flats?

"No friends allowed, either. Not unless it's my sister."

"Nobody but April. I think I can handle that." She tilted her head, a teasing smirk playing on her lips. "I'm guessing online chat rooms are out, too, then?"

He scowled and spun around, leaving his back to her as he spouted over his shoulder, "Not funny, Laurel."

It kind of was, but she guessed jokes were off limits as well. She watched him walk until he reached the end of the hall. "Does that mean I officially got the job?"

He stopped and speared her with a look that reached every single one of her senses, as if she were standing naked before him. "You can start tomorrow."

Chapter Three

Micah's phone buzzed and he barely glanced at the screen to verify it was his sister calling him back before he hit accept and started yelling. "What. The. Fuck were you thinking by sending a complete stranger into my bar to interview for a *nanny* position? Who are you and what did you do with my sweet little sister?"

"Sweet?" April laughed, her voice more raspy on the phone than in person. "Not sure which sister you're referring to, Big B, but sweetness has never been my forte."

"Right." Micah kicked off his jeans and slid into a pair of shorts, thankful to finally be home and have Shae tucked in for the night. "I should've known better when you said you were sending a friend to interview."

"Oh, come on. You know this will be a good thing—having someone who is actually good with kids watch the little munchkin instead of bringing her to work with you every day. I'm sure there's a study somewhere that proves the scent of alcohol is damaging to growing brain cells."

Micah shuffled to the kitchen, grabbed a beer from the fridge, and popped the top. He wasn't sure "good" was an appropriate word. Nothing "good" could ever come out of someone he didn't know taking control of the very thing he loved most in the world. His father had taught him that lesson. His father had also taught him how to super glue stab wounds to not lose too much blood. The only difference between him and his father now was Micah had never been his father's everything. Alcohol had—a whole warehouse full of it that he'd entrusted to someone he thought he knew. So strangers to Micah meant trouble, and he still couldn't wrap his head around April's friend starting as his nanny tomorrow. What exactly had he agreed to?

He swigged his beer.

April's voice filled the line again. "Laurel said you left before you two could figure out the details. Were you calling to get her number? Or better yet, I can just walk over to her room."

He had left on quick notice. A phone call from Russo for another deal. And the thing with working for an associate? Saying "no" or "hold on" simply wasn't an option.

"Actually, I was calling to give you a piece of my mind," he said with a light tease in his voice. "But I suppose I'll talk to Laurel too." Having set hours for Laurel to watch Shae, Micah had realized during his last job of the day, wasn't going to work because of Russo's inconsistency and short demand for his presence. Micah didn't like the idea of keeping someone in his home, but the more he thought about it, the more he knew it was the best option. In his home, Shae would be safe. And he'd be able to check up on her any time he had a free moment.

April's footsteps tapped along the wooden hall. He'd been to his sister's room a few times while helping her move in. It was tiny, with only a pull-out bed and a small sink— the bathroom shared with other residents on her floor and therefore grungy as hell. He heard a door open and April mutter something to the side of the receiver, and then another voice came onto the phone.

"If you're calling about the background check, I won't have it to you for a few days. I ordered it, though, if that counts." At the sound of Laurel's sugary sweet voice, the image of the blonde-haired beauty standing with her impeccably round tits staring at him through her drenched shirt flooded his brain. The perfect size for his hand, which meant it was more than convenient that Laurel was going to be watching Shae while he was *gone*. Being around her for only fifteen minutes today had already awakened his tamped-down libido. Prolonged exposure to her was sure to be damaging.

"That's fine," he told her, running his finger down the condensation clinging to the neck of the beer bottle. "I was calling to discuss living arrangements during your time of employment with me."

Laurel coughed. Or choked. "Living arrangements?"

"I've been to the house you and my sister rent from. And while it's in a decent neighborhood, I can't see how a room that small could possibly be big enough for a six-year-old to run around in."

"Oh."

"I'm also not comfortable with her being around your roommates. I don't know them."

The line fell silent. Then a chair or bed creaked with her movement. "I guess I hadn't thought of that. I suppose I can watch her at your place."

Micah plopped down onto the couch and tipped his head back, closing his eyes from the hazy, yellowed ceiling light. "Which brings me to my next concern. Because of my involvement with the bar"—or Russo, but he wouldn't ever tell her *or his sister* about that part of his life—"there will be times when I'm called in late at night or on emergencies and won't be able to wait for you to get here by subway or taxi, so I'd like you to stay here for the summer."

*H*is place? For the whole summer?

Laurel glanced up to April. Did she have any idea that her brother was going to propose *living* with him?

April tipped her head to the side, a strand of chin-length brown hair brushing along her red-stained lips. "What?" she mouthed.

Pressing her hand to the receiver, Laurel whispered, "He wants me to move in with him!"

April shrugged, not looking at all surprised at her brother's request. Had they talked about this? Had her friend *okayed* it? "A little weird, I know," she said, lowering to the edge of the bed. "Especially because *eww*, that's my brother. But it makes the most sense."

Laurel lifted a "hold on" finger to April then raised the phone back to her mouth. "Um…Micah? Can you give me a second? Your sister is trying to tell me something."

"Take your time," he responded, and Laurel couldn't tell

if his noncommittal tone was supposed to be sarcastic or not. A tiny reminder that moving in with a complete stranger was sure to be more than a little awkward.

"How so?" she asked April.

"Well…" She ran her fingers down the heavy crease in her black pants, ticking her reasons off one finger at a time along her thigh. "It'd be pointless to pay rent on a room you're hardly going to be using. If you don't have to commute back and forth, it'll save you money on transportation. Plus, the more Shae's around you the better. That kid is seriously lacking in the positive-influence department."

Give up her room? Entirely? "I don't know," she said quietly. She'd wanted a job for the summer, not a new home to go with it.

"It's not like he lives in a mansion or anything," April added. "But it sure beats a room in a house full of people you don't even know. Other than me." She smiled brightly.

A deep voice trickled into her ear. "Hello? You still there?"

"Yeah," she told Micah, taking a humungous breath. It was a job. And it was only for a few months. April was right, too; by moving in, Micah's little girl—April's niece—wouldn't be spending her days in a dingy, dilapidated bar.

Another deep breath, and she stared at her knees as she sealed her summer fate. "Okay. I'll stay at your place."

Chapter Four

The pad of Laurel's finger hovered over the doorbell for another moment. What the heck was she doing? Sure, she needed a job, but giving up her rented room to move in with her best friend's brother? The man whose intimidating presence scared the bejesus out of her?

What if his little girl didn't like her? Or worse, what if this very job proved she wasn't fit to be a caretaker?

No. She planted her feet in front of the door, locked her knees. Taking care of kids was her thing. She'd always been good at it. Besides, she thought to herself, April had said Micah wasn't as scary as he looked. *He's just a little rough around the edges.*

But rough meant he could fire her, and then who knew how long it might take to find another room or apartment she'd be able to afford. With no job.

Ugh, her mind had been whirling full speed since meeting with Micah at the bar yesterday. This whole situation exhausted her, and her appreciating the fact that she already had a secure job for the fall. *I just need to make it a few more months…*

Laurel shook out her hand then pressed the button.

The door opened faster than she was ready for, Micah filling the entire space wearing a tight T-shirt and jeans that led to his bare feet. Jesus, he looked more like an MMA fighter than a single father who'd hired her as his nanny. Two solid black bands tattooed around his forearm just below his elbow held her attention for a moment, then the words scripted beneath: *DON'T TERRIFY THE ROUGH ONES.*

A warning to others, or a reminder to himself? She wasn't sure she wanted to know.

"You actually showed up," he said and swung the door wider. "Guess I owe April twenty bucks."

Is that what he thought of her, that she was one to not stick to her word? Or flake out? That sent a hot rush to her ears. So much for first impressions. She bit her tongue against the variety of comebacks she wanted to throw at him, forced a smile, and said, "I'll make sure she buys me a coffee, then."

His eyes scanned over her shoulder to the street behind her for a beat, then he pointed to her suitcase. "Want to get that inside?"

To where she was going to be living for the next few months? She tried not to think about the awkwardness of the situation and nodded. "Sure."

He moved into the living area and she followed, cumbersomely dragging her suitcase behind her. Three steps and she was in, almost halfway through the whole room.

"A little small, sorry," Micah said, shoving his hands into his pockets. "Fine real estate is hard to come by in these areas." It was a joke, based on the pursed-up grin he shot down at her. It didn't make her toes tingle. No, that was just her nerves. Nerves that were suddenly zipping and zapping like a current of electricity through her body. Up, down, around… *Oh, jeez. Not this again.* "Anyway…" He ran his hand through his hair. "This is the living room."

She stole a quick glance: TV, small end table, purple couch— Wait. "You have a purple couch?" She almost laughed. "Really?"

His face tightened, but though it was barely noticeable, something in his eyes changed. Relaxed. "It's what I get for letting a six-year-old choose the color. Shae wanted glittery pink pillows to go with it, but a guy's gotta draw the line somewhere." He winked at her, and the unexpected casualness of the gesture made the room tilt off kilter. "So we put them in her room and got black with flowers instead."

Purple couch, flowered pillows… The more Laurel glanced around the room, the more she realized he must have let Shaelynn help with the decorating. A framed picture of colorful butterflies hung beside the TV, and the beige window coverings were tied with ribbons that looked more like they belonged in a little girl's pigtails. It wasn't a bachelor pad at all, as she'd imagined while lying in bed last night.

Laurel was still trying to soak in all the details of the room when Micah twisted and stepped into another room, extending his arms out to his sides. "The kitchen."

Another glimpse around the room revealed an L-shaped counter along the far wall adorned with only a microwave, coffee maker, and small two-burner portable stovetop. Between the lower cabinets, where it looked like there should've been an oven, sat a mini refrigerator, the glass doors showing off two shelves stocked full of beer.

"No oven?" she asked, scanning the rest of the room. Full-size fridge against the stark-white apartment wall on the side, a circular table in the corner, and…that was about it.

Micah shook his head, eyes on the mini fridge. "Oven broke a few months ago. Management wanted hundreds of dollars to replace it. But who uses an oven, anyway? This is much more useful."

Beer instead of home-cooked foods. Apparently his bachelor side was here in the kitchen. Following his gaze to where all the beer bottles sat—the fridge missing any sort of lock—she couldn't resist. "You keep the knives out of reach, but your six-year-old has eye-level access to all that alcohol. Seems like your concern for safety is a bit skewed, don't you think?"

The air around her shifted as he turned to face her. She wanted to look. She didn't want to look. Sheesh, had she ever met anyone whose size intimidated her so much?

He planted his feet, leaning closer to her, *towering* over her. "Can't say it affected me as a kid." A pause, a blink of a second to let his *don't tell me how to raise my child* tone settle beneath her skin. It did; the man was scary as hell this close, but she also caught a hint of a wobble in his words. Like maybe he didn't fully believe them himself.

Micah and April's mother abandoned them when they were little; April had mentioned that when they'd first become friends. Laurel didn't know anything about their father, but suddenly she wanted to. As if it might help her understand him better.

She opened her mouth, but before she could get anything out, he said, "How about I show you where you'll be sleeping," and walked out of the kitchen, gesturing for her to follow.

Silently, she trailed him, her suitcase bumping along the carpeted hallway. With each step, she catalogued what she knew of him so far.

Right foot. *Raising six-year-old alone.*

Left foot. *Has taken some precautions in keeping Shaelynn safe, but might need some help with that.*

Right foot. *His backside is really,* really *nice to look at.*

Left foot. *I wonder if those muscles under his back pockets feel as hard as they look—*

"It's only a two-bedroom apartment," he said, suddenly coming to a stop. The movement was too fast, and by the time her brain caught up, she was already slamming into the back of him. Right against the butt she'd been staring at.

Oh my god.

He twirled fast and clamped his huge hand around the top of her arm to steady her, those brown eyes ticking from her eyes to her forehead to her ears, mouth, over her shoulder, then back to her eyes. The force of his stare triggered a nervous giggle from her lips.

"I'm so sorry," she said, forcing her gaze to stay with his even though the intensity was making her a little dizzy. "I didn't expect you to stop right there."

"We're at the end of the hallway," he said, unamused.

Right. But... She pointed to where the carpet dead-ended. "I couldn't see because of your..."

Butt. Not a chance she'd admit that.

Your entire ginormous body blocking my view. Yeah, not that either.

"Because of...um, you," she said, swallowing down what

she hoped was all of her embarrassment.

He stared at her. She pinched a polite smile. Then he swung open the door to a tiny room flooded with pink… everything. Curtains, rug, blankets on the twin-sized bed. From beneath the pink dust ruffle on the bed, a blonde head peeked out, big eyes skirting directly to Laurel.

"Princess," he said to the girl, "this is Laurel. She's a friend of Aunt April's and she's going to be staying with us for the summer to help watch you."

The girl eyed Laurel for a minute, from her leather sandals all the way up to the plain white tee she'd thrown on this morning. Shaelynn propped a naked Barbie in front of her and pushed the doll's arm up and down to wave at her. "Hi," she said, scrunching her button nose into an adorable grin.

"Hi," Laurel answered back. "Did we interrupt Barbie getting dressed?"

"No." Shaelynn wiggled the doll. "This is Pickles, and she always walks around naked." A quiet giggle echoed across the room. "Daddy says she's crazy."

Micah chuckled, his grin still beaming. It was the first smile she'd seen from him, and the warmth of it — the love and adoration for his daughter in it — liquefied her completely. A big, scary man disarmed by a giggling six-year-old.

Huh.

"As I was saying," he turned and said to Laurel, "it's only a two-bedroom apartment, which means you can keep your things in here, but I'd like you to sleep on the couch."

Wait. *What?* "Sleep on the couch? You're teasing, right?" she said, her voice wavering as she scanned the rest of the hall. Two doors. His room and likely a bathroom. The

apartment was small—most in the city were, but even so…
"I guess I assumed I'd be getting my own room. Or at the
very least have a bed to sleep in?"

"And *I* assumed," he responded, his voice hinting at a
lightness she didn't know someone as sobering as him could
have, "that if I told you your own room wasn't an option, you
wouldn't agree to move in." He took the handle to her suitcase and dragged it into the room. "The couch pulls out into
a bed, but if you're that opposed to it, you could always sleep
in my room." Something dark and almost desirous flickered
in his deep brown eyes, and he clutched the handle, waiting.
Ridiculous as it sounded to her, she couldn't tell if he was
joking or not.

Ten minutes. The tenacious—yet goddamn beautiful—
blonde had been in his apartment for ten whole minutes
and she was already cleaning.

Micah peeked at Shae, sitting beside him on the couch.
Shae stared back.

"It's not like our place is a pig sty or anything…," he
whispered. But the harrumphs and sighs coming from
whichever room Laurel was in seemed to indicate otherwise.

Shae shrugged and giggled. "She's really pretty, like
a mermaid. Only out of the water and without wearing
seashells."

*If mermaids have tight asses and curves that scream to
have hands run over them then, yes, she's just like one.*

Micah smiled at his daughter and tapped her nose. "Not
as pretty as you, princess."

"You think she'll clean the bathroom too? I made a big mess in there this morning with the toothpaste."

A bag of trash suddenly landed at his feet, and he tapped his daughter's leg. "Answer your question?" He glanced up as Laurel tugged on her yellow, plastic gloves then brushed her messy hair off her face with her arm. A tight white shirt clung to her slim figure, giving him a front-seat view of her tiny waist and handful-size tits. Tits that would fit perfectly in his mou—

"Can you take this to the Dumpster?"

Micah pointed to her scrunched-up nose, the way two little wrinkles on her forehead mirrored the disgusted look. "Is it really that bad in here? I straightened up right before you showed up."

She blinked down at him, her expression slackening. "Oh…um. I didn't mean… I just thought I'd make myself useful."

Useful? He fought the urge to roll his eyes. What had his sister gotten him into?

Afternoon turned into evening, and after a pizza delivery, an inch of water on the bathroom floor from Shae's bath time "waterfall," and a stack of bedtime stories, Micah was beat and finally ready for bed.

"I'm going to turn in for the night," he said to Laurel, setting a handful of blankets and a pillow on the couch beside her. He pointed to her book. "Feel free to watch TV if you get tired of reading. The place is small, but we're used to the noise."

She'd changed into a tight gray tank and some cotton shorts, and Micah couldn't help running his eyes over the milky smooth legs that were crisscrossed over his couch or the scooped neck of her shirt that hit at the perfect angle for him to steal a peek at what lay beneath.

Regardless of the way she'd buzzed around his apartment today—scouring, wiping, polishing—he couldn't deny that this woman's body was absolutely stunning. One he wouldn't mind spending a few hours with between the sheets.

Carefully, Laurel dog eared the page and set the book on the side table. "Thanks, but I'm pretty tired too." She stood and started sorting through the blankets. He reached past her to pull out the bed then unfolded a sheet and tucked in its edges.

"I have a few rules for Shae," he told her, positioning the pillow at the head of the bed. Laurel dropped the pile of blankets at the end of the mattress, her thin frame facing him. His hands itched to settle in the crook of her waist, just to see what it would feel like.

She smiled up at him, her hair in a bunch to one side. "I figured you might."

Had he come across as that type? If he was honest with himself, he hoped like hell he had. Shae was all he had, and he wanted to make damn sure that when she wasn't with him she was in the safest of hands. "I don't expect you to stay locked up in the apartment, but I need you to keep the outings with her minimal and on this side of town only. The library, park, places like that."

Laurel nodded. "That's manageable. Do you want me to text you every time we go somewhere?"

His instinct was to say yes, but one thing he'd learned over the years in working with Russo and his mob was that they couldn't be trusted. If something went down with one of his deals and Russo or any other associate got ahold of

Micah's phone, he didn't want a single one of them knowing Shae's whereabouts. Not that they didn't know where he lived—they were the mob; they knew everything—but one less piece of information wasn't going to hurt. "That won't be necessary."

"What about allergies?" Laurel's blue eyes connected with his. "Does she have any, especially to food that I need to know about?"

"No."

"Allergies to medications? Some kids are—"

"No," he said again, flattening his lips together. Why hadn't he thought to go over all of that with her? He'd never left Shae with anyone other than Ryan, and Ryan didn't need briefing. He'd been around since the very first time Micah had laid eyes on Shae. His best friend knew everything about her.

Suddenly, the fact that Micah was going to be leaving his baby girl with someone he had only known for less than a day started to prickle at his skin and sink through to his bones. Micah had never been one to panic, but... Could he trust Laurel with Shae? What if something happened?

A dainty finger tapped his arm. "You look worried," Laurel said to him, at the same time shaking her head. "Don't be. I've been around kids all my life. I'm trained in CPR, and I've had a few psychology classes. You can trust me."

Psychology wouldn't protect Shae, and that's where his mind kept catching. As Laurel's hand drew back, he snatched it into his, wrapped his fingers around hers.

Her lips parted, a small burst of air filling her lungs and widening her eyes.

Warm.

Soft.

He really shouldn't be thinking about smoothing that hand over his chest and running it down to where his blood was likely to pool should he step any closer to her. Smell the hint of soap left over from her shower.

"Those are just words," he said, his thumb swiping along the back of her hand. "Trust, in my book, is earned through actions."

The buzz of his phone startled Micah from sleep. Jesus, was Ryan throwing work at him already? He peeked at the screen of his phone and groaned when he saw April's name.

"I hope whatever you have to say," he mumbled into the phone, "it includes an explanation of why you sent a female version of Mr. Clean to move in with me."

"Cleaning already?" April whistled. "Wow, she didn't waste any time, did she?"

"My apartment is spotless," he told her dryly.

"Are you seriously complaining that someone cleaned your shit?"

"I'm complaining because it's a little more than awkward moving in a complete stranger. And I'm blaming you. Besides, I had to play maid to this so-called nanny yesterday." He eased his legs off the side of the bed and sat up, rubbing his face. "Why are you calling me so early?"

"Ease up, Mr. Grumpy. I just wanted to make sure you didn't act like a big, scary monster on her first day. She was a little nervous when she left yesterday, and I know how you can be."

"Nervous about watching Shae?" His baby girl could be stubborn at times, but otherwise was no trouble at all.

"No, about being around you. I believe the first impression you gave her was that you are—and I quote—*a scary sex god.*"

A sex god? "Seriously?" The startled look on her face when he'd walked into the women's restroom flashed through his mind. He laughed. Yeah, scaring people sort of came naturally for him. But had there been something else, too? An underlying attraction to him?

By the way she'd been scowling yesterday while cleaning, he doubted it. He glanced at the clock. "Listen, I have to get ready for work. Is that all you wanted—making sure I didn't damage your favorite roommate?"

"She's more than my roommate; she's my best friend. Just be nice to her, okay?"

Yeah, whatever. "Hey, Ape. Do you really think I'm a horrible father? Is that why you set this up?"

A breath of silence beat past. "Not horrible," April finally said. "And Lord knows you're a much better parent than I'll ever be. I just think maybe having a woman around will be good for the munchkin."

A woman around… He still didn't know what he thought about that.

After a shower, Micah made his way into the kitchen for a quick cup of coff—

"What the hell is this?"

Across the countertops and on the floor was a sea of brown paper grocery bags.

Laurel spun from the opened—and now full—pantry

cupboard. "Oh," she said, sounding surprised. "Um…food? You know, from a grocery store? You didn't have anything besides sugary cereal for breakfast." She smiled carefully.

"We usually eat at the bar." He narrowed his gaze. Why did he feel the need to defend himself? It wasn't like he cared what she thought of him. Even though she was right, because when was the last time he'd had time to cook anything? Did that make him a bad father? Damn his sister and her meddling ways—now he'd be questioning everything he did with his daughter.

"That's what Shae said." No reproach in her words; so much different than the woman who had questioned him for letting his daughter hang out at work and for replacing his oven with a beer fridge.

He stood in the doorway and watched as Laurel continued unloading food into the fridge: oranges, burgers, pizza, wings… Juice, she'd even bought juice.

"Sit down," she said after the bags had been emptied. "I'll make you breakfast."

"Breakfast?"

Laurel tilted her head with a small smile. "Yeah, that meal people eat in the mornings?" A tiny laugh bubbled from her lips as she worked at the counter, her back now turned to him.

He sat, and Shae bounded into the room. She plopped down next to him at the table, grinning up at him. An intricate braid twisted her thick blond hair across her forehead and around the side of her head, where it draped like a curtain down her pink-and-white…*dress*?

Shae smoothed her hair. "Laurel did my hair like a real princess. And she got the wrinkles out of my dress."

"Ironed it," Laurel amended her, working quickly with a bowl and spoon.

Shae beamed. "She ironed it. Don't I look pretty, Daddy?"

"Prettier than pretty," he said automatically, but in his mind he was trying to recall the last time he'd done more than run a brush through his daughter's hair and found an outfit that semi matched.

Two bowls landed on the table in front of them. Steaming oatmeal—smelling sweet and foreign in his poky, little kitchen—stared back up at him.

"Yummy!" Shae yelped and reached for the plate of fruit Laurel had added to the table. Blueberries, sliced banana—

His stomach tightened, and Micah shook his head. "I can't eat that."

The two girls in the room froze, their eyes as big as quarters. Then Laurel started to fidget. "I should've asked what you like. I'm sorry."

The last time he'd eaten oatmeal was when he was a kid, living off his mother's welfare checks in the months before she abandoned him. Cooked on the stovetop with butter and cinnamon, just like what was sitting in front of him. No way in hell was he going to eat it now. He shoved the bowl away from him, the ceramic screeching on the wooden table like nails on a chalkboard.

"It's really good, Daddy," Shae said around a mouthful, completely unaware that his chest had all of a sudden collapsed like it was being steamrolled. "Put some blueberries in it." Shae finished off her bowl and asked for another. Laurel, without saying a word, scooped more from the glass dish into her bowl. A home-cooked meal… Hell, if there was a way to make him feel like a shitty father, this was it.

Abruptly, he shoved away from the table and headed for the door, the sudden need to punch something very hard coursing through his veins. "I have to get to work."

Outside, with the chilly morning air clinging to his bare arms, he slid his phone from his pocket and texted Russo.

Hands are getting twitchy. Got anything today?

His response was almost immediate.

Only if u like twins, LOL.

Twins? Micah didn't want to ask. He just wanted to beat the shit out of something.

Chapter Five

"Okay, spill it," April wrapped her freshly manicured hands around her mug and said, her voice echoing along the brick walls of the coffee shop. "I need details on your first day. Are your hands raw from all that scrubbing?"

Laurel lowered the glass of iced tea from her lips and cocked an eyebrow, stealing a brief glance at Shae, who was coloring at the kiddie table a few feet away. "Please tell me you're guessing that's what I did because you know me so well instead of talking to your brother *about me*."

Coffee Bean and Tea Leaf was practically empty, only one group of elderly women near the door, but Laurel still hoped her friend wouldn't say something out loud that would embarrass the heck out of her.

A smirk lifted April's lips and sent hair-like crinkles out from the corners of her eyes. "I might've talked to my brother this morning. He said you started cleaning the minute you got there. Were you really that nervous?"

"How could I not be? If he wasn't your brother, I'd be a little scared staying with him." Laurel let out a giggle then sighed. Finally she had someone to talk to about the whirlwind she'd been through in the last twenty-four hours. Giving up her room, moving in with Micah, being around *him*. "He's a tad intimidating."

April's lips pursed out then in. "A tad?"

"Okay, more than a tad." Especially when he touched her. Or ran his eyes over her body like he wanted to touch her. Yeah, that wasn't something she would ever tell April, though. Sisters didn't want to hear about their brothers that way. "Plus, I don't think he likes me very much."

"Doesn't like you? Sweetie, no one could not like you. You're too…*you*." The long front pieces of her bobbed hair swayed with the shake of her head. Laurel remembered when April had cut her hair that way—a spur-of-the-moment decision a few months ago after they'd shared a bottle of wine to celebrate her new job with Luxury Skincare. *New job means new hair!* Her brown hair and the way the cut of it now framed her high cheekbones gave her that edgy, Victoria Beckham look.

Laurel sipped her tea and frowned. "Regrets hiring me, then?" An understatement after this morning when he'd stormed out over oatmeal. "I don't know. I just feel like, one, he isn't happy that I'm there and, two, he doesn't trust me."

April propped her forearms on the table, her gold bangles clinking together. "Micah's always been slow to earn trust. It'll come once you've shown him you're fully capable of taking care of Shae. As for him not wanting you there? That's because my brother doesn't like people he doesn't know in his private life." She shrugged with a smile. "He just needs to warm up to you. Give him a chance."

Give him a chance to warm up to her?

Laurel sank farther into the purple couch and stole a bottomless breath. She could do this. Right?

His footsteps sounded in the hallway before he emerged, still wearing the T-shirt, jeans, and black boots he'd left in that morning. She tried not to take in the way his shirt clung to his muscles or the tip of another tattoo that peeked out from the collar of his shirt, but failed miserably. The man was gorgeous, from the way his brown hair hung shorter on the sides and longer in the front to the day-old stubble on his otherwise smooth face.

His chocolatey brown eyes roamed over her as he entered, an embarrassing reminder that she was staring at him. "Thanks for getting Shae ready for bed," he said quietly, obviously in an attempt to not wake his now-sleeping daughter. "I can't remember the last time she was actually asleep before"—he glanced to his watch—"eleven."

"Eleven o'clock? For a six-year-old?" Had they gone to bed that late last night? And what else did he let her do—watch rated-R movies? The thought horrified her, but worse was the hardened expression pointed at her.

Warm up to her... Judging him on his parenting skills likely wouldn't help. She shook her head and pinched a smile. "I mean, you're welcome. I'm glad I can be here to help." She set aside her book. "Are you hungry? I can warm up a pizza."

"Ate at the bar. Thanks, though." Micah collapsed onto

the couch with a giant sigh, and a bubbly tingle shot through Laurel with his unexpected presence. Like her blood had suddenly become carbonated. His humungous frame filled the entire space beside her, encroaching far past the middle of the couch. Unnerving. Intimidating.

Silence pressed in on her as he tilted his head back and rubbed his forehead. Without his menacing height, he definitely looked less scary. More…drained, and like a dad who was working his butt off to provide for his daughter.

She peeked at him again. His face was downright contradicting, as if whoever created him was at war with the type of guy he was intended to be. The strong angles of his bone structure contrasted with the soft, alluring appeal of his lips. They seemed harmless and inviting compared with the severity of his features and the greenish bruise stretched down the side of his jaw. *Wait…another bruise?* This one must've been a few days old, and looked as if he'd been punched in the face. How had he gotten that? And on his hands, an assortment of cuts and gashes littered his reddened and swollen knuckles. Cuts from working at a bar… Broken glasses, maybe? She pointed to his hands then, realizing he wasn't looking at her, cleared her throat. "Did you get in a fight with Jack and Jameson?"

Unexpectedly, his head snapped up, eyes cutting and narrowed. On her. "What did you say?" It was more of a growl than actual words, and the harshness of them zapped her body with the immediate impulse to scramble away. Or scream. If he weren't her best friend's brother, she might have screamed.

She sank farther into the couch and gestured to his hands. "You have a lot of cuts on your hands…and a bruise

on your face…and I was making a joke about your work—
you know, the names of alcohol?"

It took him a minute to piece together her words. Hands.
Work. Joke. Then he pinched his lips in an unattached smile
and ran a hand through his hair. "Unloading deliveries can
be a bitch sometimes," was all he said. Flat and uninflected.

Maybe it was best not to talk about his work. But if she
was going to get him to warm up to her, and if she didn't
want to feel so awkwardly unwelcome, she needed to try
something else.

With a slow exhale, she twisted in his direction and
reclined against the armrest for support, crossing her legs
in front of her. *Breathe, Laurel. And remember what April
said—he's not as scary as he looks.*

Easy for her friend to say.

"I was thinking," she began softly, slowly, testing the
words in the quiet room, "about taking Shaelynn to the museum tomorrow. She told me today that her kindergarten
teacher read a story about dinosaurs at the end of the year,
and it's been proven that what children experience in real
life is better remembered than something in a book." Laurel
stopped because of the funny look he shot her—tilted brows
and a straightened mouth; a complete look of bemusement.
Had she been talking gibberish?

Mentally, she shook her head. It was just something
she'd learned from her parents growing up—instead of reading about the forest, her parents had taken her camping. To
further understand the oceanic food chain, her family had
planned a summer vacation to the beach. Obviously, he'd
lived a different life than she had. "Anyway," she continued,
"if you're not working, you should come. You know, like a

normal family outing?"

His eyes squinted harder, jaw ticked— If looks could kill, his would've filleted her in half like a chicken breast. He ground out, "*We* are not a family."

Right, they weren't. Nevertheless… "I know, but I can tell your daughter adores you and the time you get to spend together, and I think she'd really like it if you came." Her words bristled him—she *knew* this by the look he shot her. But that same look was also misfiring the synapses in her brain and scrambling everything into a big, messy pile of I-don't-know-what-to-say-or-think-or-do. Ugh, she hated how flustered just sitting near him made her. Laurel bit her lip and smiled across the couch at him.

Micah's expression grew harder, his eyes darker. "I didn't bring you into our home so you could point out everything you think I'm doing wrong as a parent." He sat up, gripping his hands around his knees as if he was all of a sudden trying not to punch something. "There's nothing wrong with the way Shae and I have been carrying on these past few years. We've gotten by just fine without *normal family outings*." The words were there, but the sureness to them wasn't. Different than the uncertainty of her watching him. This seemed like it had nothing to do with her at all.

"I…" No words came. How was she supposed to respond to that? "I know," she said weakly. "I was just suggest—"

"Well, fucking don't." Sharp and cutting, and then he sprang off the couch and slammed the door to his bedroom.

Laurel closed her eyes. *Warm up attempt: FAIL.*

Chapter Six

His knuckles were pounding. Why the hell did Russo keep sending him to complete and utter douchebags who found it entertaining to try and fight back?

Try. At least that was *all* they did.

Micah wiped the bloodied backs of his hands on the underside hem of his T-shirt one last time, then opened the door to his apartment. The sound of giggles—both his daughter's and someone else's—boomed from the other room. Immediately, he smiled; his daughter's laugh had always been so contagious. Its warmth and bubbliness held the ability to erase the shitty part—or...most days...*parts*—of his day instantaneously.

Seeing Shae's meddling little nanny, on the other hand, tied a clump of knots in his stomach. Having her in his space, commenting on how he'd been raising Shae, wasn't exactly what he'd had in mind when he'd offered her the job.

Hot air blasted him as he stepped farther into the living

room and dropped his keys onto the table, that clump in his stomach rolling over and tangling tighter. When he was here, under the dissecting eye of Laurel, he just wanted to get out. But when he was away, spending his hours at the bar, and even when dealing with Russo's guys, his mind drifted back to her. The way he would catch her eyes running over him when she thought he wasn't looking, the nervous fidget that would take over her body when he was anywhere near... He was attracted to her—who wouldn't be with her impeccable figure and full lips worth kissing?

But that was all it was: attraction.

He threw his wallet onto the table with his keys just as his daughter screeched, "I'm a sparkly fairy! And my fairy dust will make you fly!"

"Shaelynn, no—" Laurel's voice followed, but then she was laughing. Hard. "I'm going to get you, you sneaky little fairy!"

What the hell?

Micah crossed the living room in a few steps and stopped short when Shae and Laurel shuffled across the kitchen, wrestling over a shaker bottle of glitter. On the breakfast table, a display board lay flat, pictures of dinosaur skeletons and descriptions scattered about. And glitter. Lots and lots of glitter.

"Daddy!" Shae shouted and started for him, ditching the glitter container in Laurel's grasp. "Look how shiny I am!" Tiny, colorful dots shimmered from every surface in the kitchen—the floor, countertops, even the fridge. A complete mess, but how could he resist smiling at his little girl, all covered in pink-and-purple sparkles?

"Are you making fancy dinosaurs?"

Shae crumpled her face. "Dinosaurs aren't fancy, silly. Just the border. It was Laurel's idea."

Micah glanced to Laurel and immediately she stiffened, her chin dipping downward. "I didn't realize it was going to turn into a glitter storm. Sorry. I promise to wipe it all up." Then she tugged Shae's arm toward the bathroom. "Why don't you get cleaned up before dinner? Wouldn't want glittery spaghetti."

"Oh, yes, I do! I do!"

Laurel shook her head, her nose wrinkled. "Then when it comes out, you'll have glittery...you know what."

Shae's eyes brightened and she opened her mouth—obviously ready to agree to producing shimmering shit, but Laurel spoke first. "No chance, missy. Get going."

Without complaint, Shae pranced out of the kitchen, her long hair and a cloud of glitter sprinkles the last to leave.

For a second Micah just stared. Had his daughter ever voluntarily run into the bath? "She usually fights me on bath time," he said, a haze of fuzziness pressing in on his thoughts. Seeing Laurel caring for Shae, interacting with her like a mother would, did something funny to his chest. Something he wasn't sure he liked.

He opened the cabinet to retrieve a broom, but Laurel snatched the handle before he could and said, "Well, I told her she could shower like a big girl. She was pretty excited about that."

A shower instead of a bath. Why hadn't he thought of that?

He took the broom from her, the sweet, floral scent of her skin blasting him with the movement. One breath, one measly inhale, but it was as if it had magical powers. One breath that cracked some of the hard tension solidifying in his chest. Tension that had been there since the moment Laurel arrived.

He looked at her.

She looked back at him.

"I can help you clean up," he said, leaning past her for the dust pan. His arm brushed her shoulder. She tensed but didn't pull away, her blue eyes skimming over his face.

Her lips pursed into a small smile, then she shook her head. "You just got done with a full day's work. You really don't need to."

It had been a full day, in more ways than one—beginning with an incomplete delivery at the bar and ending with Russo's cluster-fuck assignment. But this was his apartment and his daughter, and he couldn't just sit back and down a beer while this woman cleaned in front of him, weekly salary or not. The place was an absolute disaster, and he wasn't that much of a dick.

"I want to," he said coolly then took the broom from her again and started sweeping the glitter into a pile on the floor. Laurel stared at him for a moment, frozen with her arms hanging loosely at her sides and gaze following his every move. Man, he'd have loved to ask what was running through that spirited little mind of hers. But he still didn't know her, and asking what someone was thinking seemed much too intimate for the place they were in. Strangers.

When he swept past her feet, she finally startled into clean mode, first setting the display board off to the side then wiping the counter with a damp sponge. The two cleaned in silence for a few minutes, but soon that silence budded into an uncomfortable level and thoughts began to swirl and turn through his mind. Russo's guys had shown their faces at The Alibi twice this week. A reminder to let Micah know that eyes were on him, that no matter how well he performed on the job, one slipup would cost him. Times like that he wished he'd never followed in his father's footsteps. Wished he'd known about Shae before signing his life over to the mob in blood. Had he'd known Emily would get pregnant then dump his daughter on his doorstep, Micah would've avoided going to the mob for money in the first place. But now he was stuck, not because he needed the money. But because the mob had a strict policy about who they let leave and when.

Micah's father hadn't gotten out until he'd lost his mind to booze and became no longer useful to them. He cringed at the thought of him doing the same.

Plastic bristles scraped the tile floor as the understanding played out in Micah's mind. If he wanted to keep Shae safe, then he was going to have to make it work with Laurel, which meant having a conversation with her that didn't end with him yelling or storming out.

"So…," he began, "you haven't had much of a chance to tell me about yourself." Glitter in the trash, broom put away, he started with a wet paper towel on the sparkle-covered cabinets. "I know you met my sister in college. And that you're going to be teaching in the fall, after you spend the summer with me…here."

Her busy arm worked quickly, a band of toned muscle wrapping the length of it. "I've spent the last two months looking for a summer job. Daycares, preschools, but it seems like no one wants to hire someone who's only going to be around for a few months." She shrugged and rinsed out the sponge.

Leaning against the counter, he ditched the crumpled towel and folded his arms over his stomach. "What made you decide to be a teacher?"

"The kids." Her eyes brightened, an unmistakable air of excitement lifting her expression. "Trite as it sounds, I want to mold our future. One kid at a time." She smiled, and it was the most genuine smile he'd seen on her yet—one that reached all the way up to her eyes.

"That doesn't sound like something you chose to do simply because you *wanted* to." The implication was clear; an aim that high didn't just come out of nowhere, and she turned away—proof that he was dead on—to rinse the sponge again.

Micah watched her hands as she gently squeezed the sponge over and over—a mundane sort of task, yet mesmerizing in the way her slender fingers swiped away the tufts of glitter—and then the stretch of skin on her neck as her long ponytail slid over her shoulder with the movement of reaching for the towel. Slowly, she dried her hands then turned to face him, mirroring his stance against the opposite counter—arms folded over her middle. Her mouth opened and then closed, and Micah stayed quiet, waiting to see if she'd have the courage to say whatever was on her mind.

He had to admit, over the last two days he hadn't been the friendliest person to her. He supposed he could change that.

Laurel cocked her head to the side. "You seem different tonight."

One eyebrow lifted. "As in…?"

"As in…" The tip of her fingernail tapped the inner crook

of her elbow, and she met his gaze straight on. "You seem not as, um, on edge?" Her eyes widened as if she couldn't believe she'd said that then added, "I mean, I just—"

Micah laughed. "You mean I'm not being an ass? Well, don't get used to it. Must be all this princess glitter messing with my brain cells." He winked at her, at the same time noticing that under the washed-out kitchen light, a single speck of glitter twinkled from her cheek, right beside the corner of her mouth. "I guarantee it won't last long," he said, and she giggled.

The sound caught Micah by surprise. Soft. Yet uninhibited. It made his insides tingle. It made him feel lighter. It made him not care that he was stepping forward, crossing the room, moving closer and closer to her. She braced her hands on the edge of the counter, her eyes never once straying from his, and inhaled a short breath when his finger gently swiped the granule off. This close, he could see the streaks of gray in her eyes, could tell that if he tucked her into his chest her cheek would rest directly over his heart.

Laurel froze, blinked up at him, then grinned shyly. "I'm sure I'll be finding glitter in my underwear for the next few days," she said beneath a giggle—this one much quieter and accompanied by a pinkish flush to her cheeks.

Underwear…underwear…underwear…

One simple word, but hearing it come out of her mouth obliterated the entire room in an instant, until all he could see was her.

Her blonde hair. Flawless skin. Full lips he suddenly couldn't pry his eyes away from. He slid the tip of his finger down her neck and ran it across the scooped neckline of her shirt, her warm skin brushing along the backs of his fingertips.

Briefs or thong?

Simple white or black lace?

What kind of underwear would she wear, and what would she look like in them?

In the distance, he heard the shower turn on. The echo of Shae's voice belting out the chorus of her favorite song accompanied the open and close of the shower door.

Micah's finger twitched, the urge to tug out the edge of her shirt and find out for himself what lay beneath. Instead he leaned down and whispered in her ear, "You are so fucking gorgeous."

Laurel blinked. Had she heard him right? She couldn't tell because since he'd touched her—first on her cheek then her jaw and then in a line only an inch above her breasts—her heart had exploded in her ears.

The huge man that less than twenty-four hours ago had stormed away from her was now touching her and telling her she was gorgeous and looking at her mouth like he wanted to *kiss* her.

And the worst part? She *liked* it. A lot.

The curiosity of what it would feel like to have him kiss her senseless overruled any levelheaded thought. It also overruled the grip she had on the edge of the counter and the solid stance her feet had planted in when she'd first positioned herself opposite him.

She reached one hand up and flattened it over his chest, spreading her fingers as wide as they could stretch. The sheer size of this man was intimidating, yes, but more than that it was the biggest turn on she'd ever experienced.

His finger slowly drew a line down the middle of her stomach, and then she did the same, sliding her hand across the ripples and bumps and pleats that made up his stomach. His hand settled on the crook of her waist. Hers mimicked his.

So carefully, Micah's head tilted. He'd caught on to the game she was playing. A move for a move. Only, *was* she playing a game? Her body operated as if she'd fallen under a trance. *His* trance. Then his eyes flicked over her shoulder, fixed on something, the corners of his mouth pushing into something that looked like a grin.

Not saying a word, he reached past her then produced Shaelynn's bag of pink candy pop rocks she'd gotten from the museum gift shop. He unfolded the top and poured the remaining pieces into the palm of his hand. By the casual way he moved about—tossing the empty bag behind her, lifting her up to the counter with one arm, stepping between her legs—it was like he did this sort of thing all the time.

"If I didn't know any better," Laurel said, fighting back a giggle. Wait, why was she giggling? Her boss stood mere inches from her face, his body pressed between her spread legs. That should matter to her, right?

Most days it would have, but at that moment, with his intense stare and hand cupping around her neck, she didn't care. Not. One. Single. Ounce.

She swallowed and continued. "I'd think you were going to pin me down and make me eat those."

Micah appraised her for a long moment, the hand with the pop rocks still and hanging in the space between them.

He shook his head, an uncharacteristic gleam in his eyes. "What fun would that be if I didn't get to taste them too?" In one graceful swoop, his hand swung up and dumped the tiny pieces of candy onto his tongue.

Immediately, Laurel frowned. "Or you're just going to eat them in front of me."

"You want some"—he cradled his hand around her head and lifted her chin with a nudge of his thumb—"come and get them." He leaned closer, she leaned in, and no thought or consideration or mere brainwork transpired before her mouth pressed into his.

Instantly, his lips parted and her tongue dove in and she didn't know who this person was, devouring candy from the mouth of the man who was paying her salary.

In little strawberry-flavored bursts, the candy exploded against her tongue. One by one, bit by bit, with Micah's mouth growing hungrier and hungrier the more she tasted. Tiny vibrations shot through her body, ricocheting down her limbs and back, then pooled in her belly.

This kiss, and the combinations of sensations that came with it—Micah's skilled tongue stroking softly against hers, his gentle lips, all punctuated by the mini eruptions—was something a girl like her would never forget.

Pop rocks were her new favorite candy.

Strawberry was now her favorite flavor.

And she didn't know how she was ever going to face her boss once this was over.

Obviously that didn't stop her. Not even a tsunami could have stopped her at this point. The candy dissolved, the sizzling in their mouths dying out, but Micah showed no sign that he was ready to back off. With one arm he pulled her to the edge of the counter and held her firmly, his other hand tightening along the crown of her head. His fingers pressed into her scalp and a tiny part of her hoped the tips of his fingers would leave an indentation. That way she'd know kissing him really happened.

His tongue worked hers, taking occasional breaks to taste another part of her body—her jaw, her ear, the hollow of her neck. With every new place he explored, the tingles in her belly sunk lower and lower.

She wanted him to touch her there.

She didn't.

For the love of everything holy, she had no idea what she wanted—

Suddenly, the water to the shower shut off, and Micah pushed away from her, his chest rising and falling with rapid breaths. Stepping back, enough so that the heat of his body and scent of his skin was nowhere near hers, he cleared his throat. "Do you and Shae have plans for tomorrow?"

A hand fluttered to her neck in an attempt to tamp down the wild thumping, and she inhaled a deep breath. "Oh... well, she begged me to take her to the zoo." Her mouth opened, the thought of asking him to join them making a quick appearance, but then thought better of it and bit her lip. "Is that okay?"

A strange look drifted over his face. Like whatever was running through his mind wasn't something he was pleased about. He folded his arms and looked her square in the eye. "I have tomorrow off," he said with a slow, friendly grin. "Would you care for some company?"

The crowded pathway circled around a bird display, the brush of Micah's elbow against Laurel's jolting her like an electric hand buzzer.

Company—when Micah had suggested joining the zoo trip, she hadn't expected to be so caught up in his every movement. Of course, she blamed the way he'd touched her yesterday. And smiled at her. *Kissed* her—

Sheesh, she really needed to stop that. She knew why that kiss had happened. He'd had a long day at work and then come home to a disaster—thanks to her brilliant idea to use glitter on Shae's project—and all of that, on top of the fact that he'd shown up with a set of fresh bruises on his knuckles, probably just jumbled his thoughts into thinking she was something she wasn't. Besides, he had hired her to watch his daughter, which automatically attached a "hands off" sign to her. Even if there had been a flood of sparks between them during that one incredible, yet completely inappropriate, kiss, there was no way he would act on it again.

Her either, now that she thought about it. Getting involved with someone she couldn't have a relationship with…that was a big no in her book. Nevertheless, knowing this man was off limits—on top of knowing a gentle smile existed beneath his scary scowl—had her refusing to step away from the source.

Bumps of his elbow. They were just bumps.

"Can we see the giraffes next?" Shae asked and skipped up the walkway, narrowly avoiding an elderly couple searching a map.

Micah tucked his hands into his pockets—*thank goodness!*—and called out, "Whatever you want, princess."

"I want cotton candy too!"

"We can have it for lunch, if you want."

Did the man ever say no to her? The two of them walked side by side and trailed Shae as she followed the picture signs, Laurel itching to put in her two cents: Letting Shae have a treat while at the zoo was one thing, but for lunch? "If I didn't know better," Laurel said in an effort to not take him to task on his decision with Shae. Things were still new, and the day so far had been pleasant, and one thing she knew was that relaxed Micah was much easier to be around than scowling Micah. She smiled and looked up at him. "I'd say you're enjoying this."

He shrugged noncommittally but glanced sidelong at her, one corner of his mouth pushing upward. Not even a half smile, but enough to trigger a dance in her belly. That mouth had been on her last night—her lips, her neck, oh god she was doing it again. At least he wasn't looking straight at her, wasn't able to see the way she couldn't stop her eyes from constantly moving back to *that mouth*. "It's nice to get away from work for a few hours," he said, his gaze scanning the path ahead of his daughter.

Work…a single word that drew up a single thought. He'd questioned her about her future, but she hadn't asked a thing about him. She tucked a stray piece of hair behind her ear. "How long have you owned The Alibi?"

Barely noticeably, he tensed—the thin material of his shirt tightening against his biceps. But his face remained staid. "Ryan and I worked as bartenders there while we were in college. The owner was a family friend of Ryan's, more like an uncle to him, and when he died of a heart attack, he left the bar to him. After the first few months, Ryan realized running a bar was a lot of work, so he asked me to co-own it with him."

"Wow," Laurel said, watching Shae as she stopped to peek in a small cage that sat alongside the walkway. Some sort of bird exhibit. "I would never have guessed. How long ago was that?"

Another pause, another clench in his arms. "A year before Shae was born."

Which would mean for the last seven years—and all of Shae's life—he'd been working long hours. Most likely dragging his daughter to the bar, too.

"Is it what you want to do?" she asked, feeling her chest tighten with the question, her heartbeat thumping against it. Or maybe that was because of the scowl he was now pointing at her.

"What are you doing?" He leaned into her personal space, though it was nothing like the closeness they'd shared last night in his kitchen. His eyes grew darker as he ground his teeth, a vein pulsing down the side of his neck. It was a look she imagined he'd give to troublemakers in a bar. Not her, his nanny.

She opened her mouth to answer, but his gigantic frame stepping closer—towering over her—cut short any words.

"I don't know you," he grit out, his tone low and deep and much scarier than if he would've yelled the words. "And you don't know me. So stop pretending you do."

Laurel pinched her lips, feeling the pressure of her brows cinching together. He didn't want to get to know her. Either that, or he was scared to. And she didn't see how this job would go over if the two of them weren't able to have a civil conversation about the things that affected Shae—including the things he did in his past and his desires for the future.

Throwing her shoulders back, she lifted her chin and looked him directly in the eye. "Well, isn't that what people do...get to know each other?"

"Not me." Two words, sharp and biting. Were they meant to scare her? Get her to stop challenging him?

Ha! If only he knew his reaction was doing the opposite. Maybe it wouldn't have been that way if they hadn't kissed. If he hadn't called her gorgeous. But he'd crossed a line last night, which meant she had no reservations crossing one now. Daggering look or not.

She cocked her head to the side, but whispered, "Because you're scared?"

"Because...," he started then stopped, the single word hanging in the air between them. Slowly, his eyes searched her face, and with every second that passed, another one of his features softened. He was so beautiful when he wasn't grimacing. "Because I'm not used to this," he finished, pointing at her.

A nanny? Being at the zoo with her and Shae? Or walking around with her, acting as if they hadn't had a Pop Rock make-out session while his daughter had been in the shower? *I have no idea what you're referring to, Micah.*

"You're not used to help with your daughter," she said anyway. It didn't take a genius to figure that one out. Though, what was meant more as a question, came out sounding like an accusation.

"My best friend and my sister are the only two who've ever watched Shae, but that's not what I meant."

Then what did you mean, Micah? Because this closeness and smelling you and knowing your hands are just inches away from me is about to make my heart explode.

He leaned closer, lowered his voice so the people walking past wouldn't be able to hear. "I'm not used to...*this*." He gestured to the diminishing space between them. "The questions." The dark look he speared her with sent the tiny hairs on the back of her neck springing up like an army standing at attention. A warning. And an intimidating one at that.

The curiosity surrounding those last two words—*the questions*—suddenly blossomed to an unhealthy level. And it had her speaking before she really knew what she was saying. "No questions about anything? Or just you?"

Why did she care about him? That question lingered in the back of her mind as she stood there, staring up into the intensity of his eyes. Sure they had kissed, and sure it was undoubtedly the best kiss she'd ever had, but this was a job. One she couldn't risk losing.

She had to give it to her mind. Great way to be realistic. Although, nothing about the jittery, fluttery, jumpy feeling that overcame her every time he looked at her was realistic. It was the kind of feeling that only happened in make believe.

"April never told me you were so nosy," he said, easing a step back. The space made it easier to breathe. She stole a replenishing breath.

"I'm just trying to understand you."

"Well, *don't*."

She held up her hands, palms out. "Fine, asking you questions is off limits." They were just words...words her mind couldn't quite grasp, because she was already searching for clues as to what he was trying to keep from her. She forced a smile, feeling oddly disappointed at the growing space between them. "I guess I can handle that. But if we're making requests, I have one too."

"A bargainer. My sister didn't tell me that, either." His arms lifted out to his sides, a tight, yet amused, pinch to his lips. "Lay it on me."

Her eyes found Shae, who had turned from the bird cage and was watching them, creases crinkling out from the corners of her eyes. "Can we just have a normal day at the zoo? For Shae?"

Seconds ticked by, drawn out and far past the moment of becoming uncomfortable. What would *normal* mean to him? Getting in her bubble and intimidating the heck out of her? Or knowingly sending her insides into a flurry?

Micah's eyes flicked to the large wooden sign standing tall above them. TAKE A PICTURE WITH THE TALLEST ANIMAL ON EARTH. Underneath the severe look in his gaze, something twinkled. "Normal," he muttered beneath a quiet chuckle and a shake of his head. "Baby girl," he called out to his daughter. "How would you like to pose with a giraffe?"

Shae bounced up and down, clapping. "Let's do it now!"

Micah speared Laurel with a look. "Is that normal enough for you?" Exacting and dangerous, but laced with a playful glint, and Laurel had no idea what to make of it. He started up the walkway, leaving Laurel frozen on the pathway.

Am I ever going to understand this man?

At the ticket booth, Micah paid the fee, and an attendant directed the trio to step onto the platform where several zookeepers held out long branches of *Acacia* over the railing. One by one as the zookeepers shook the branches and called out names, giraffe heads started popping over the barrier.

Shae shrieked with a giggle and tugged Laurel next to

her. "Don't let them bite me!"

Laurel's heart was all over the place, especially filling that hollow spot at the base of her throat. Micah's words and the closeness of him… *You asked him for normal, which means you have to act that way too.*

Laurel blew out the tightness in her chest and crouched down to Shae's level, hands on her knees. "Pretty sure we won't have to worry about that once your dad steps up here. Giraffes don't like big, scary, tattooed men."

They both snickered then Shae shook her head. "My daddy isn't scary. He sings songs to me at night."

All of a sudden, Micah lunged between them and gently pinched his daughter's lips together. "You little stinker, that was our secret."

Through her pressed lips, Shae's tongue shot out and licked Micah's fingers. All three laughed then straightened at the photographer's signal for the picture.

"Mom," the man behind the camera said, glancing to Laurel, "you'll need to stand behind your daughter and closer to Dad. Giraffe will be coming in on your right."

"Oh," Laurel blurted, "I'm not—"

"Right next to him," the man added. "Closer, closer…"

Laurel opened her mouth to explain, but the zookeeper guiding over the giraffes spoke first. "Hurry." Laurel snapped her mouth shut and positioned herself as the man directed, careful to keep her arm from brushing Micah's.

"A little more…" the man coaxed. Laurel hesitated. Jeez, weren't they close enough? Mere inches separated his bare arm from hers. Micah's eyebrow rose. *Normal enough now?* his amused eyes seemed to say.

The woman with the giraffes jiggled the branches. "You

only have a second. They're losing interest!"

In fear of ruining the picture and disappointing Shae, Laurel jumped closer to Micah and bounced right off his huge chest. Reflexively, he swathed his arm around her waist, his gigantic muscles both steadying and swallowing her. Then the camera's shutter snapped.

Sticky fingers circled Laurel's wrist, and then her hand smashed against Micah's. Skin on skin. Palm to palm. There went the composure she'd gained over the last hour.

"You need to hold hands with Daddy so we don't lose you," Shae said, sugary sweet as the pink cotton candy in her grasp. The scent of it reminded Laurel of strawberries. Of Pop Rocks. Of Micah— No, she wouldn't go there again. "The train ride has a lot of people."

"Sweetie, you won't lose me," Laurel rushed out, her words sounding more like a whinnying horse than a convincing caretaker.

"Besides," Micah said to his daughter, "how am I supposed to steal bites of your treat without both hands?" He pretended to swipe at the ginormous mound of fluffy sugar and missed. His other hand, though—the one cradled around Laurel's—held firm. And although the afternoon sun was shining bright over the expanse of the animal park, the warmth surrounding her hand sent a tingly shiver up her arm. When was the last time she'd held hands with a man? Touched a man, even?

Way too long. Obviously that was why April had given her The Tickler.

Shae ripped off a hunk of cotton candy and thrust it at her father. "I'll feed it to you, silly." Granules of sugar floated through the air and stuck to Micah's T-shirt as she jumped and attempted to shove the piece into his mouth. After several tries, cotton candy covered his shirt and chin, looking more like a stuffed animal had exploded on him.

Laurel laughed, glancing side to side as families passed by. What did they think—seeing the huge, tatted man she'd first seen walk through The Alibi's door standing in line with two girls and cotton candy all over him? Did the sight of him unnerve them like it did her? Make their feet twitch with the urge to run away from him?

Micah glanced to Laurel with a childish grin, so genuine it disarmed her instantly. "A little help here?" he said, pointing to the mess on his shirt.

Or maybe that twitchy feeling in her feet was the urge to run *to* him?

She lifted the hand he still had clutched around hers. "I'll probably need this back, then."

"No," he said immediately, a small shake of his head. He was still smiling, and that darn smile was like a magnet, pulling her closer. "It's crowded." His thumb swiped over hers. "Wouldn't want to lose you."

A swarm of dragonflies stirred in her belly. *Oh.*

Laurel had no idea what he was doing. If it was all a joke to appease his daughter's earlier request or something more.

Not something more. Couldn't be.

So why, then, when she ran her fingers delicately over the front of his shirt, plucking off puffs of sugar one by one from his shoulder to the center of his chest, did she suddenly feel so flushed? Like she'd been dipped in molten hot lava?

Because cleaning your boss's shirt was never included in the job description.

Once at the front of the line for the kiddie train ride, the attendant directed them to sit three to a seat—straddling one in front of the other, their feet dangling onto the imitation wheels. "A bit of a squeeze for your family, eh?" the attendant spouted before moving on to the next family in line.

A squeeze? More like a sandwich with Shae sitting in front of Laurel and Micah behind. *Right* behind. So close she was pressed completely against his chest, his thighs tight alongside hers. Warm. Firm. Solid. *Oh dear.* The nearness did funny things to her insides, wringing her nerves and igniting her libido, and that realization suddenly had her cheeks heating.

As much as she could in her tiny sliver of space, she turned to Micah and mouthed "sorry" with a crumpled-up expression. His playful air was gone, replaced with the muscle of his jaw clenching just below his ear. Not mad, but more like he was…holding something back. Before he could respond, the train jerked forward and started its tour through the African Savannah section of the park. Laurel let out a startled yelp and gripped onto Micah's knees.

"Maybe I should've told you guys," she said, glancing side to side as the train picked up speed, "I'm kind of scared of things that move fast!"

Animal-scented air blasted her face. Crowds of people whizzed past, and suddenly a solid hand planted on her waist and secured her body to the one behind hers. "You won't go anywhere."

Cramped in the tiny space, so focused on the fingers holding tightly to her, Laurel's heart climbed into her throat and settled there. How long was this ride going to be?

"Scared of things that go fast," Micah spoke into her ear, once the speed of the train stabilized. "A childhood fear, I assume."

Laurel shook her head. "More like an after-high-school fear. I was in a car accident with some friends the summer before I went to college. Driving too fast on a curve in the rain... Nobody was hurt too badly. I got the worst of it being in the passenger seat where the car hit the tree. But, I don't know...I've never been okay with going fast after that."

His finger traced a line down the side of her forearm and along the inside of her wrist to the thin white scar. "This is from the accident?"

She nodded, trying not to get caught up in the feel of his touch. "One of the tree branches came through the window with the impact. I'd had my hand up to protect my face."

The train swerved down a dusty line across the replica desert, throwing Laurel's rear back and forth like a ping pong ball between Micah's thighs.

Zebras, giraffes, lions... The ride had promised a view of all of these, but the overwhelming presence behind her—pressed against her—kept Laurel from seeing any of it. His hard chest holding strong to her back. His muscular thighs embracing hers. And his...bulge rocking into her rear with every bump and turn.

It was awkward.

And uncomfortable.

But really, really...*hot*.

Micah tried to ignore the back arching against him, the slice of smooth skin that flashed as Laurel's shirt lifted with the movement, the images flashing through his mind of her legs wrapping around him—images he *should not* have about his daughter's nanny. He wanted to touch her. He wanted to pull her closer and feel that sexy-as-hell body against his. The urge consumed him, so much that he hadn't realized the ride was coming to an end until the train shuddered to a stop, Laurel's ass vibrating against his cock. He couldn't help it—a torturous groan sounded out of his lips.

They peeled themselves apart and off the train car.

"Ooh, penguins!" Shae shouted, already running for the cave-like entrance. *Yes, something cold would be awesome right about now.* Laurel smoothed her shorts, letting her long hair cover her face. And then they walked in silence toward the exhibit's entrance.

Cold air blasted his face and neck, but even as they followed Shae deeper into the dark building and past the informational displays about the variety of penguins, Micah couldn't gain control of the way his body had reacted. He was on fucking fire, and there was no way to quench it.

If this had been any other girl, he'd already have made a move—pulled her into a poorly lit alcove and kissed her senseless. But this was his daughter's *nanny*. His *employee*. And getting mixed up in that would no doubt end in disaster. He'd already crossed a line with the way he'd been unable to resist her last night after work.

He kept walking, looking for anything that could help erase the feel of her rubbing against him. The penguins in their enclosure; grandma and grandpa shuffling past...definitely not the woman beside him, who apparently wouldn't look at him either.

Shae ran up to the enclosure and smashed her face against the glass. His body so wound, he started for his daughter, but then—*fuck it*—he snatched Laurel's wrist, tugged her into a darkened recessed area, and lowered his face merely an inch from hers.

"The next time," he said, low enough that only the two of them would hear, "you press your body against mine like on that train, I will strip you bare and pleasure *every* single part of you..." He leaned in close to her ear. "With my tongue. I will make you scream my name until it's the only word you can speak. Are we clear?"

Her warm breath on his neck, followed by a tiny whimper that sent his blood flowing south, was the only response he got.

"Good." With his teeth, he nipped at her bottom lip then said, "I've got to go to work." He retrieved some money from his wallet and pushed it into her front pocket. "In case you need a cold drink." Lord knew he did.

Laurel's wide-eyed gaze turned suspicious as she watched him say good-bye to Shae, promising to be home in time to tuck her into bed, though she was smart enough not to call him out on his lie—that he'd had the day off from work. Technically, from the bar, he did.

He gave her one last searing look, wishing to hell that he could claim her mouth and see if she tasted as good as last night.

Micah kissed his daughter's forehead then blew her one more kiss from the doorway, thankful the light-less room didn't allow Shae to see the knuckle-sized gouge on the side of his head. Curled into a ball on her bed, Shae caught the imaginary kiss and tucked it under the covers. "Just in case I wake up scared," she said, rolling onto her side with a yawn.

"Daddy's here, which means there's no reason you should be scared. Good night, baby girl."

In the kitchen, Laurel stood facing the sink, a scrub brush in one hand and a pot in the other. The woman pre-pared a full meal every night. Sure, the food was great, not to mention good for Shae to have more variety than what was offered at The Alibi, but what would his daughter expect once school started back up and it was time for Laurel to go? Micah didn't know how to cook past microwavable noo-dles and PB&J sandwiches, and the sudden realization that his daughter would grow up on foods that most likely didn't provide the essentials she needed to be healthy pressed a sickly fizz into his stomach.

For a moment, he stood watching the delicate muscles in Laurel's back gather and crinkle beneath the thin white straps of her tank top as she scrubbed the pot. Tight black stretch pants—*leggings?*—covered her bottom half, provid-ing Micah with a full-access view to the perfectly formed ass that lay beneath. One that no amount of gym time could give, but must have been graced by the man above.

Damn, that wasn't going to help the battle his mind was fighting, the guilt radiating throughout him not simply be-cause he was staring at her, but for how it was making him feel. Because this fascination with Laurel—the way his mind continuously wandered around thoughts of what it would feel like to pin her naked body beneath him—was going to end up costing him.

Just like earlier today, when one of Russo's guys had landed a fist of brass knuckles to Micah's temple. The scrawny-but-quick dickface had been prepared, and Micah hadn't because his mind was stuck on the memory of Laurel's ass pressed against him on the kiddie train. The feel of her trapped between the wall and him, even her slender hand in his.

He'd hooked up with women since working for Russo, though none of them had ever interfered with his focus, ever been a distraction that put him in danger. Laurel was an itch he desperately needed to scratch, to expel this fascination with her out of his system, so next time one of Russo's guys didn't pull something more deadly on him.

"Laurel," he said, resting his shoulder against the wall.

"Oh!" The dish brush flipped into the air then landed with a *clink* against the pot. Quickly she spun around, her hand flying to her chest, but the moment she laid eyes on him, a slow smile pushed up her lips. "I'm sorry. I was so caught up in my head I didn't hear you come in." She brushed her hair back from her face with the side of her arm. "Are you hungry? We had chicken and mashed potatoes. There's some left over in the fridge."

"I'm not hungry," he said, sliding into the room. His blood pumped harder, the familiar predatory feel to the way his feet moved with purpose. Only this taking wasn't for money. This was all because he'd had one taste of her and his mind wouldn't shut the hell up about taking another.

Micah took three deliberately slow steps toward Laurel and she stopped smiling because, holy heck, he was seriously intimidating. Whenever he was in the same room as her, his presence took up too much space. So much that it pressed her against the counter, squeezing the last traces of breath out of her.

As he closed the space between them, his eyes drifted away from hers and scrolled from her neck all the way down to her feet. Everywhere his gaze focused, she felt it, like his eyes were hands skating over every inch of her.

This wasn't what she had planned when taking the job from him. Feeling so overwhelmed with...*attraction* to him. With the strange flustered feeling in her chest every time he came into the room. With the knowing that her body was really starting to like him.

As he stalked closer, a reddish splotch on the side of his head caught her attention. Blood. "Your head..." She rushed up to him and stood on her tiptoes to better see. "Micah, how did this happen?"

Up close, the rich scent of man and *him* and—*oh, my gosh*—something she wanted to bury her face in all night long knocked her dizzy.

Seriously? Did all women react this way around him? Or was it just her and her pathetic boyfriend-less stint?

Micah set his jaw and grit his teeth. His eyes flicked over her shoulder as he muttered, "Bar fight."

She poked her tongue into her cheek, tilting her head at the same time. "In the early evening? Someone drunk enough to start a fight at that time?"

A crease appeared on his forehead and she couldn't tell if it was a result of confusion or fascination. He said nothing.

Her breath bottled up in her chest. Jeez, why couldn't she just breathe normally when she was this close to him? "I mean…," she said, "…I can help you clean it up so it doesn't get infected." She turned for the sink, but he snatched up her wrist.

"Laurel, I don't want leftovers." He slid his hand up her arm, tracing over the scar she'd told him about earlier. "And I sure as hell don't want to be mothered." Bit by bit, he lowered to her level, eyes meeting hers as if he wanted to gauge her reaction as he whispered, "All I've been able to think about since this afternoon is if you always taste as amazing as you did last night." Gently he placed a lingering kiss on her cheek then slid his mouth to her ear. "And I intend to find out. Right here, right now."

His hand slowly trailed all the way up her spine until he was fingering the back of her neck, scorching hot as if every single part of her he touched was branded with *him*. His fingers pressed into the base of her neck, his mouth no more than half an inch from her jaw. So close it was impossible to tell what was feathering her skin—his breath or his lips.

She wanted to tell him to go ahead. To take whatever he dang well pleased, because let's face it, she hadn't been able to get past that kiss either, but her voice was stuck somewhere in her throat and her breath had vanished clear out of her chest and was this how people had heart attacks? From the anticipation of a kiss?

Eyes locking on hers and never once leaving her face, he unhurriedly slid his mouth closer and closer. Every millimeter, her heart doubled in speed, and it wasn't their first kiss—wasn't the suspense of not knowing what his lips would feel like. The beating in her chest was knowing exactly what his kiss felt like and wanting—no…*craving*—that feeling again.

What would she crave if they'd gone farther than just a searing hot kiss? What would his burning touch feel like somewhere else on her body?

His mouth continued sliding toward hers, and her heart continued jackhammering in her chest, and then there were only three millimeters left. Then two. Then one.

It wasn't fireworks. Wasn't any kind of magical explosion. When his mouth covered hers and his tongue parted her lips, it was more like she was dying. Like this kiss was the very breath her lungs needed, and if she didn't get more she would shrivel up or suffocate or, she didn't know, *die*.

The thought was ridiculous, and Laurel knew she probably looked like a half-drunken, lust-crazed woman right now, but she couldn't help it. All day long, her body had been twisted so tight, thoughts of Micah and his words about stripping her bare to pleasure her haunting her every move.

This was a really bad idea—kissing her boss. But right now, all she needed was release and if he was willing to give it…

He tugged her closer, guiding her backside to the counter with a few broad steps. She felt so tiny in his arms, so helpless against the rage of sensations that blasted through her with his every touch. With the steadfastness of his fingers as they weaved into her hair and tipped her head back so he could deepen the kiss.

His tongue stroked hers, weakening the strength in her

legs. *Christ, this man literally makes me weak in the knees.* She wound her arms around his neck, pressing her body closer to his. He used the leverage to lift her to the counter, placing her rear just along the edge. With one hand he separated her legs and stepped between them, the heat of his body and the caress of his tongue clamping her insides even tighter.

Wrong as it seemed, a wild, untamed, *dangerous* buzz zipped through her.

He felt dangerous.

And she liked it.

The unfamiliar ache in her body craved more of his touch, of the way he memorized her with his fingertips, as if he needed to trace every curve, to imprint the contours of her body into his memory. And then his fingers slipped beneath the straps of her tank, tugged them down past her elbows to expose her bare breasts.

"What about Shae?" she leaned back and asked. "What if she comes out for a drink?"

He shook his head. "I set a bottle of water by her bed. She won't be coming out."

He'd planned ahead… So he'd known he was going to do this? *I wonder what else he's planning to do.*

Micah licked his lips, the sight of his tongue snaking between his lips every bit as predator-like as the feel. "A nanny with exquisite tits. Who'd have thought?"

Her cheeks warmed instantly; no man had ever said something so blunt to her before.

"These are mine for tonight."

Or that…

He ran the backs of his hands down her cheeks.

"And I want to see this pink turn to red when you come

and scream my name. Do you think you can manage that, Laurel?"

Oh, as long as he kept saying her name in that throaty tone, she'd definitely be able to handle that. His finger swept over her mouth, lingering long and slow on her bottom lip. A whimper escaped, and instead of answering him, she arched her spine toward him, a salacious grin taking over her mouth.

He let out a soft chuckle. "I see," he said, pinching her nipple between his fingers and rolling it back and forth until it pebbled, "we have the same thing in mind." One simple touch, accompanied by his whispered words, and her body lit up like a flare, flickering with pulses of the need for more. He worked one breast, cupping and kneading, and just when the over-attention started to drive her mad, sending tingles past her waistband, plummeting low into her belly, he slid to the other side. At the same time, he took her mouth, his lips and tongue driving in unison.

Drunk on lust—there was no other way to explain the unsteady, lightheaded fog slowly sinking over her. Gasping for breath, she broke away from his mouth. "More—"

Wait. No. *Oh my god*, had she really just begged her boss for more?

"Don't worry," Micah said, his lips traveling down her neck. "I intend to do much, *much* more with you." His tongue circling her nipples, one after the other, slowly he dragged her leggings down her rear and legs and threw them to the ground. The cool rush of air chilled her skin, but then he sucked one nipple into his mouth, and she burst into fire. Burying his head between her breasts, he licked and kissed and squeezed. Her fingers grappled through his hair, search-ing desperately for a way to scream out that he'd tripped her wire and she was putty in his hands. He wasn't even touching between her legs yet and she was already throbbing with the need for pressure. She wound her legs around his middle and squeezed them tight, so tight that the feel of his rock-hard erection beneath his jeans was somewhat of a relief. A strained groan floated into the space between them and burst a wave of confidence over her. So he was desperate for release too?

"I want to know every inch of you," he muttered, his lips against her collarbone. "I want to kiss you from head to toe. But first…" One finger slid beneath her lace panties and drew a single line along her folds. "I want to taste this."

So demanding. And the words shot through her fast and hard, like the sudden pop of a Champagne bottle. Yes, she wanted that too.

His teeth grazed the skin across her chest. "Is that all right with you, Laurel?" By the insatiable glint in his eyes, she had a feeling it wasn't proper permission he was looking for. And she didn't care. She just wanted to be closer to him, to drown in his musky scent and the feel of his mouth on her.

"Okay," she said breathlessly anyway.

"Good." Like a man on a mission, he gripped the sides of her panties and slid them down her legs then added them to the pile of clothes. Her whole body blazed like a live wire; her blood, her bones, her nerves were all singing with the need to feel his mouth between her legs.

A fluttery, empty feeling trembled in her belly as he firmly planted one hand on her knee. He lowered and kissed the inside of her leg, from behind her knee up her thigh. A vicious shiver centered all her wants and wishes and desires into one location. The very place he was inching closer and closer to.

Could the man move any slower? Her hands laced through his hair and tried to pull him in. Close the distance. Oh god, she'd never wanted something so fiercely before.

"Hmm, then again, this is moving pretty fast," he said, pausing just before making contact with her center. Warm breath and the whisper of his stubbled cheeks brushed against the hypersensitive skin inside her thighs. "I vaguely remember you saying moving fast scared you." One eyebrow lifted. He grinned. "Am I scaring you right now, Laurel?"

She glanced down at him and his mischievous smile— one she wasn't used to seeing on his typically staid face. Scared? The only thing that scared her was the idea of him not finishing what he'd started. Quickly, she shook her head.

"And this—" He licked a long, slow line up her middle, rapid-firing all of her senses into one, big ball of mush. "Does *this* scare you?"

Torture. *This man is complete and utter torture!*

"No," she said. "Please, just…" Finally, he brought his lips to where she wanted him, smearing that last word into several syllables as it became a moan of pleasure. He grabbed her backside, cupped her cheeks, dragged her closer, and even if she'd had her hand over her mouth, she would have never been able to stop the second moan.

Laurel collapsed back onto her elbows, her head and neck craned against the wall beneath the cupboards. Had she ever been this vocal before? At this point, did it really matter? Her synapses were going all wonky, and she was pretty sure if he did that again she'd be incapable of remembering her own name—

His tongue swirled and dipped and licked until she was

thrashing around on the counter. Her legs extended over his shoulders, but because of her position, not able to stretch out or arch back, the coiled-up pressure just kept building and building until she thought her body would burst out and cave in at the same time.

Then his finger slipped inside her. And another, penetrating to the very spot that made it impossible to breathe. Beneath the ricocheting beat of her heart in her ears and panting she couldn't slow, the low-but-whispered words "Come for me, Laurel" caressed her. His lips covered her nub and sucked. "I want you to come on my tongue." Fingers deeper, tongue lapping and zigzagging and— "I want to taste you in my mouth long after I go to bed."

She gasped, as if his words held the key and had just unlocked the ability to let go. The orgasm rocked her body, stole her breath, her mind and everything in between. It reached her fingertips, her toes…radiated all the way through each and every cell. Like she was floating, and would be for days.

Panting, she closed her eyes, until the trembling of her legs and beating of her heart faded into his gentle, warm kisses working their way back up her middle.

"That was the most beautiful sight I have ever seen." Micah leaned over her splayed body, took her face in his hands, and kissed her. He tasted of him, and he tasted of her, and on any normal day the thought of this type of kiss would've had her worrying about the cleanliness of the situation or the appropriate way to decline, but the combination of the two—his and her essences—impelled such a passionate and uncontrollable force that left her feeling weak-willed and wildly courageous at the same time.

She reached between them for the button on his jeans,

but a hand clamped down over hers. "Don't," Micah said firmly, still with his mouth lingering over hers. His brows pushed together, tiny crinkles creeping out from the corners of his eyes. He pinched his lips and inhaled a slow breath through his nose, almost as if there was some sort of war going on inside his head. "Tonight was your night."

Slowly, he returned her tank straps to their proper position then bent to retrieve the rest of her clothes. They landed in a pile on her lap, and then he turned and headed for his room.

My night?

Chapter Seven

"Can you come?"

He most certainly could, especially with the scent of his sexy little nanny lingering like a cloud around him, the glorious taste of her still on his tongue.

Micah shifted under his down comforter when he heard the squeaky voice again.

Wait. *Squeaky?*

His eyes popped open just as Shae threw her tiny body on top of him, sprawling like Superman across his bed. "Daddy, please say you'll come." A waterfall of long hair showered over his face, and he pushed it back to reveal a wide, toothy grin. "Please, please, *please.*"

Not that he could ever say no to his princess, but he at least had to find out—

"Where is it you're going?"

"Laurel is taking me to the park again."

"Again?" He rubbed his face. "When did she take you

before this?" He knew nothing of them going to the park. He'd told Laurel she didn't need to check in with him every time they left the house, but the sudden thought of his baby girl vulnerable to whatever dangers lay in the open, and very public, park twisted his stomach into a ball of knots.

"The other day," Shae answered, squirming impatiently. "Will you come? Pretty please?"

He grabbed his phone from the nightstand and glanced at the screen. No text from Russo. It didn't mean he was off the hook for the whole day, but maybe he could steal an hour or two with Shae. The Alibi's responsibilities could wait too. Surely he'd hear from his partner about the inventory and stocking that needed to be done, but his daughter was more important.

"Yeah, baby girl," he nudged Shae off him and said. "I can go with you. Let me take a shower first, okay?"

Once showered and dressed in jeans and a T-shirt, Micah made his way to the kitchen where Shae and Laurel stood at the counter, preparing pasta salad and bagging cut-up fruit.

"Do I have time for a cup of coffee first?" he asked as he entered the small room. His eyes went directly to the counter Laurel had been sitting on last night, his cock jumping with the memory of her stunning body propped up on it like a goddamn queen. Maybe hooking up with her wasn't the best idea, and maybe it was sending the wrong message about him to her, but there wasn't an ounce of regret in what he'd done. If anything, it had him craving more.

He glanced to Laurel. Cut-off jean shorts and a fitted, but not too tight, T-shirt. He'd explored every inch of skin that lay beneath that material, and he wondered how the day was going to go, spending it with the woman he couldn't stop imagining naked and trembling beneath him—

"Here, Daddy. Laurel already made one for you."

Near the sink, Laurel busied herself with loading the pasta salad into small Tupperware containers. Didn't look at him. Didn't smile. Didn't react in a single way to his presence. *So this is how it's going to be?*

"Shae, honey," he said, gripping the edge of the counter to keep him from rushing over to her and kissing her breathless just to show her there was nothing she should be regretting from what they'd done. "Would you get the small cooler from the closet by your room for all this food?"

Without complaint, his daughter romped out of the room, and Micah approached Laurel with hurried but careful steps. "Is this how it's going to be?" he asked, striding well into her personal bubble. He felt her stiffen. "You not talking to me because we decided to—"

"Don't say it out loud," she whispered, throwing him a condemning look. "Your daughter can hear you right now."

He cocked his head to the side, eyes narrowed. "You didn't seem too concerned about that last night."

"Well…" She threw back her shoulders and lowered her gaze to her hands. "I'm not sure I was thinking straight last night."

A smug smile tilted Micah's lips upward, and he smoothed his fingers over the line of her jaw and neck. "That, Miss I Need More, sounds like a compliment to me." If he hadn't been standing this close, he'd never have seen the pinkish hue to her cheeks. Or the slight slant of her head when she relaxed into his touch. The very sight slammed an uncontrollable hungry surge through him.

But then she opened her mouth. "You hired me to help

take care of Shae, not do…*that*."

With a shrug and a teasing wink, he shot back, "I have no problem calling *that* one of the benefits of the job."

He wanted to taste those lips again, wanted to carry her to his bedroom and devour every square inch of her body. She licked her lips, holding her ground. Whether she regretted their hookup or not, she clearly wasn't opposed to doing it again. What they'd done was supposed to be a one-time deal—get her out of his system and move on. But this craving was potent, pressing in on him, clouding his thoughts. Slowly, he lowered to her level. He was playing with fire—pure, wanton fire—and he was all too willing to get burned. Eyes searing hers, he leaned closer…closer—

"Got it!" Shae hollered, and the two of them sprung apart like polarized magnets. The cooler landed on the counter with a staring Shae behind it. She glanced to Micah then Laurel. "Am I in trouble?"

Quickly, Laurel gathered the pasta salad and utensils. "Of course not, sweetie. I was just telling your dad about your new friend."

"New friend?" Micah questioned. His daughter didn't have many friends outside of school and the neighbor next door. How come she hadn't told him?

Shae clapped her hands and giggled. "I hope he'll be there today!"

He?

The three of them descended the wide sidewalk through the rolling expanse of bright green grass and past the pond lined with trees, their branches draping over the glistening water. Boston's high-rises stood tall in the distance, sending a pang of disgust through Micah. Had his childhood been different—his life in general—he may have ended up there: a successful businessman instead of a co-owner of a decrepit bar. He would never have met Russo or gotten tangled into the web of mob life.

"He's here!" Shae said, running ahead to the grassy edge of the pond where a flock of squawking ducks surrounded an old man. Gray scraggly beard, clothes dirty enough they could've been run through a wash of black ash, shoulders hunched with the outline of his ribs rippling the back of his shirt...

What the hell?

Micah whirled in Laurel's direction. "You let my daughter befriend a fucking seventy-year-old *hobo*?"

Laurel smiled, tucking a stray strand of hair behind her ear. "She met him the other day. His name's Charlie."

"I don't give a shit what his goddamn name is. He could be dangerous." Micah picked up his pace toward his daughter. Laurel matched his speed, her legs working twice as hard to keep up with his broad steps.

"He's not, though."

He glared at her. "And you know this how? From letting her talk to him last time?" Jesus, how could she be so ignorant? "You don't know the world like I do—the fucked-up shit people will say and do to get what they want. People are conniving and deceitful, and you can't trust any of them." Like him... Technically he was one of them. Russo's people too.

A warm hand landed on his arm and tugged against his

forward push. At the same time, his daughter's voice drifted up the hill. "…were there ducks here too? And what about the playground? Was that here?"

Micah's heart pounded in his chest, and instinctively he looked around, scanning the outskirts of the park: a mom and toddler on the swings; a few high school kids throwing a Frisbee to a dog; no one who looked suspicious or dangerous or even like the mob type.

His gaze skipped back to his daughter.

"Four hundred years is a long time ago," the old man said with a chuckle, his voice raspy with age and Micah didn't even want to think about what else. "I don't think plastic slides had been invented back then."

Shae nodded. "But ducks had been invented, right?"

The man smiled, and at the same time Laurel stepped in front of Micah. "History. That's what they talk about."

Micah scowled, his eyes flicking back and forth between Laurel and his daughter. "She can learn about that in school. From a goddamn book."

"It's good for her." Laurel splayed her hands over his chest and held firm so he couldn't take another step without barreling over her. "She's experiencing the past from someone who lived it. A textbook can't give her that." Her hands slid down his arms and worked to unclench his fists. "Besides…it's good for her to see someone who's less fortunate."

Daggers, it felt like he was shooting daggers out of his eyes. Less fortunate? Was she kidding? He'd lived the less-fortunate life, and it was nothing he wanted Shae near. "Because she's so well off? Give me a fucking break."

Just then, Shae ran up and retrieved a small tub of pasta salad from the cooler. "For Charlie," she grinned and said before running back down the hill.

Laurel shook her head. "Because it builds character. And because it's a window into the past with unfiltered access to all that knowledge." Her eyes brightened. "Imagine if kids—our future generation—had a solid grasp on life before X-Boxes and iPads and cell phones." She shrugged, pinching her lips into a small smile. "What would our world be like then?"

Saving the world one fucking child at a time. Starting with his daughter. "I don't like the idea," he said, but his words had lost their weight. As much as every cell in his body wanted to protect Shae from strangers in the world, maybe Laurel was right.

Laurel blinked. "A little trust would be nice."

He sighed. "I do trust you." Fuck. Not until those words were out of his mouth did he realize how true they were. "It's everyone else I don't trust. You don't know what kind of people are out there."

Her fingers caressed his, over the gashes and scrapes marring his knuckles. "I would if you told me." The sincerity in her voice and gentleness of her words sent an aching desire to simply…tell her everything.

"You want to know why I come home like this—" He pointed to the fairly new gouge on his temple, the one she'd tried to clean last night.

She nodded. "And this." Gentle fingers traced the cuts on his hands.

He wouldn't tell her everything—couldn't because just knowing about Russo could put her in danger. But maybe he could give her a little—just enough to make her understand.

With a hand on her shoulder, he guided her to face

the pond and sit beside him on the hill. Close enough that his daughter was still able to be seen and heard, but with enough space to whisper and not be heard himself.

"When Ryan and I took over The Alibi, the bar was in really bad shape—worse than it is now—with old equipment, furniture, basically everything. We needed a lot of money to fix it up, but because we were both still in school at the time and spending all of our extra hours in the bar, I had to pick up a side job." Beside him, Laurel looked out toward the pond, Shae in her sights. "It's an under-the-table job, one I'm pretty much stuck in."

Laurel stiffened, cutting her eyes in his direction. "You mean it's illegal." She didn't look scared, but there was a definite change in her expression and the slow, cautious tone of her voice. She gestured at his head. "Let me guess; that wasn't from a bar fight."

"No."

"So this job involves fighting?"

For a breath of a moment, he said nothing. She pulled her knees up to her chest and wrapped her arms around them, then nodded in understanding, and he had to admit, she was nothing like the innocent, naïve twenty-four-year-old he originally thought she was.

This woman had a smart head on her shoulders—a head that contained eyes that were now glaring at him.

"I don't fight for money, if that's what you're thinking," he said with a sigh. He had to be careful, not give away anything that would hint to his ties to the mob. The safety of his daughter meant keeping the nanny who cared for her out of the loop as much as possible. "I fight to get people to pay the money they owe."

"So you can then get the money," she accused, her words short and pointed. She thrusted back her shoulders and waited. Damn, she could be feisty.

"A percentage of it, yes." Below them, Shae sat cross-legged on the grass, watching the man—Charlie—as he dug his fork into the pasta salad and shoveled bites into his mouth. Laurel sat quietly, tightening then loosening her grip on her bare legs.

"So you're like…a repossession guy?" she asked.

He stared down at his boots, the scuffs and gouges along the edges of the soles he'd never noticed before. "I suppose it's kind of like that. Though the people I'm getting to pay up are mostly criminals."

She let that settle, pressing her unpainted fingernails into the skin along her forearms. Then she said, "Criminals… Is it something that could put Shae in danger?"

Micah winced with his answer, but this wasn't anything he should sugarcoat. "Yes."

"And me? Could it put me in danger too?"

He wanted to say no, wanted to assure her safety would never be an issue, but if there was one thing he wasn't, it was a liar. "If you became an asset to me, then most likely. If they found out you were responsible for Shae—which, knowing them, they probably already do—then definitely."

Behind them, the dog playing Frisbee started to bark, and Micah's senses jolted into overdrive. He cast an eye over the grassy hills, keeping his other on his daughter. The dog jumped in front of the boy holding the Frisbee and spun a circle, barking again. Micah relaxed.

"Who's *they*?" Laurel asked, staring at the side of his face. Micah pinched his lips tight, said nothing, and Laurel nodded curtly in his direction. "You can't tell me."

"It's for your own good."

Her eyes narrowed. "You mean safety."

"Yeah."

"I'm not sure I like that."

She had no idea how much he hated everything Russo could hold over his head if he didn't pull through with whatever assignment was thrown at him. A harsh-sounding chuckle sounded from his lips. "I have no say in the matter. Like I said, I'm stuck."

"What happens if you don't get the money?"

"I don't know. I've never not gotten it."

The breeze blew along the hillside, the rustle of leaves replacing the sound of their voices. Laurel shifted, straightening her legs and flattening her hands along her thighs. Her voice was lower, more stoic when she asked, "What about your sister? Does she know?"

"You sure do ask a lot of questions."

Her fingers curled under the hem of her shorts. "I'm just trying to understand."

He let out a breath. "No, April doesn't know." And he expected it to stay that way. "I don't want you to tell her, either."

"Because she wouldn't approve?"

"Because"—he speared her with a pointed look—"the only person who would approve of this is the man who raised me to be this way."

"Your father?"

Micah said nothing, feeling the burn in his jaw as his teeth clenched harder. His father didn't deserve a single breath wasted on him. Laurel stared at him for a moment, then her eyes skittered down to his forearm. "Your tattoo," she said, "*Don't terrify the rough ones…*" Her voice lowered. "That's you, right? The rough one?"

Unexpectedly, he chuckled. *Guess I never thought of it that way.* "No."

Silence. A bird swooped past, squawking out a loud, shrilling call. He glanced over at her, at the tiny crease drawing a line between her dainty brows.

"So the rough one is…?"

His chest grew tighter, stomach feeling like it was falling over the edge of a cliff. "Off limits," he snapped. No more. He was done talking. Jesus, why did thinking about it always do that to him?

Her gaze met his. "Is it your family?"

The back of his throat burned like words were screaming for release. Muscles jumped under his skin. He scowled at her. "Why are you so curious?"

"Because I want to know you better." Simple. Not sounding reproachful at all. And ever so slightly, it worked loose the tension constricting his body.

"That's a pretty dangerous wish for someone who's all rainbows and fucking sunshine, wanting to save the world." He shook his head at her. "You don't want to know me."

Her eyes searched his face. Gentle. Inquisitive. Then her finger traced the tattoo. "Is it your father?"

Fuck. Really? He swallowed against the revulsion even those two simple words—*your father*—brought up and smiled tightly. Fine, he could give her this. "*Was.*"

"Oh…" Her warm hand flattened on his forearm. "He's—"

"Not dead, unfortunately. Just out of my life." *And nowhere near Shae, thank god.*

A moment of silence descended between them, the sound of ducks protesting the lack of food in the area filling it. "Is it something you want to talk about?" she eventually asked, sliding one finger back and forth across his skin.

"No."

"Okay." Another hushed beat, this one more drawn out and awkward. Then she said, "When I was a kid, I used to play this game with my parents. They would ask me to come up with a single word to describe how I was feeling."

He arched an eyebrow. "Sounds like a boring game to me."

She shrugged. "Maybe *game* is the wrong word. But it really helped pinpoint the emotions I was feeling." She faced him, sliding her hand up his arm and across his chest. "Try it. Tell me one word to describe what you feel when you think about the past."

That was easy. "Fucked up."

Laurel laughed and nudged his shoulder with her hand. "I'm being serious."

He tried to look past the beautiful smile. The searching blue eyes. He narrowed his stare on her again, though this time he couldn't manage the starkness. "So am I," he said, softer than he'd planned.

"Please?" Fingers mapped out the cords on his neck, ran across the collar of his shirt.

"Shitty," he growled between his clenched teeth. Damn, what was this girl doing to him?

"Micah…"

"It's all I've got. My childhood was nothing to write home about, okay? It was fucked up and shitty and left me feeling the same. Now can we please stop talking about it?"

Her fingers stilled, warm and pressing into the side of his neck. He focused on the feel of them instead of the burning in his chest until she rose to her feet and said, "Of course we can. Let's play some ball." From the bag of toys they'd carried in, she retrieved a plastic ball and bat, then hollered to Shae that it was game time.

"Girls against boys!" Shae squealed up the hill.

Micah stood, hands on his hips, taking a deep breath to push down the choked feeling in his chest. "That's hardly fair. I'm outnumbered."

Shae scrunched her nose and jabbed her thumb in Laurel's direction. "You haven't seen her play."

Micah laughed and Laurel gave his daughter a playful shove. "Yeah?" she said. "Well, I wasn't lucky enough to grow up with a dad who liked sports." She looked at Micah when she said this, eyes soft in an accepting sort of way. He wasn't going to talk about his father, but she'd tell him about hers. Whatever.

"No sports?" both Shae and Micah spouted, identical incredulous stares.

Laurel shook her head. "My dad's more the artsy type. Painting, playing music. Besides, in a house full of all girls— even if he'd wanted to—sports would've had no chance." She picked up the bat—wrong hand placement, wrong stance, low elbows.

"Wow." He gestured to her form. "I know a six-year-old who holds the bat more correctly than you." Smiling, Shae pointed at herself.

Laurel's eyes twinkled. "You want to come over and show me then, hot shot?"

Hot shot? She had no idea.

"Gladly." He marched from their makeshift pitcher's mound—a small tub of pasta salad—to their makeshift home plate, which was a paper plate from their bag. "First of all," he said, swooping around to her backside. "Your stance is all wrong." He slid one leg between her thighs, using his foot and knee to spread them. That sight hurled the memory of last night and those gorgeous legs parting for him into his mind. It felt good to be back on familiar ground, seducing a woman instead of barfing up his feelings.

The rubber soles of her shoes screeched along the grass but did nothing to cover up her slight intake of breath as his legs worked hers apart. He leaned in, his mouth just behind her ear and whispered, "Keep them like that—spread for... stability."

Letting his front graze along her back, he swung his arms around her and flattened his hands over hers. "Your grip should be lower. One hand on top of the other, not much space between." Lightly, his fingertips ran up her wrists then arms, dipping into the delicate crook of her elbow. His finger swirled once, twice against her skin then from underneath he lifted her arms away from her body. "Elbows up and bent at a comfortable position." His hands continued over her shoulders then down her back, making sure to graze the sides of her breasts with the pads of his fingers. He was teasing her, yes, but the feel of those breasts—even just barely—and the strangled moan that vibrated from her throat sent his blood flowing south. "And these," he said lowly, gripping her hips with more force, "should fall into the same plane as the rest of your body." With one, painfully slow caress, he brushed his palms from her neck to her thighs.

He stepped around to face her, nodding with approval

at the stance she held. A smile tugged at his lips, his hands momentarily satisfied by the fleeting contact of her skin on his. But too soon it left him aching for more. Eyes zeroed in on hers, he reached out and cradled her chin in his hand. "Keep this tucked toward your front shoulder to give you a good view of the pitcher and the ball."

Her gaze intensified. "I don't think there'll be a problem with that."

Slowly, he picked up the ball and made his way back to the pitcher's mound.

Chapter Eight

"I just ate the fattest hamburger. Can you see my food baby?" April stood in the doorway to Micah's apartment, patting her stomach with a crinkle in her nose. She shot Laurel a teasing smile. "I should just throw up, right?"

Laurel laughed and threw herself at her best friend, not realizing until the moment she was in her arms, the scent of Michael Kors flooding her nose, how much she'd missed her.

"No food baby. You look amazing, as always. I'm so glad you came over." Laurel desperately needed to talk to someone about the mounting attraction that had been sparking between her and Micah—the way her body came alive when he was anywhere near her, the way—after their conversation at the park a few days ago—she worried for him when he left the house to "work." But that wasn't why she'd asked April to come over.

"So dish," April said, sliding her sunglasses atop her head. "How do you like the city? Met any cute guys while watching my niece? Ooh, any DILFs at the park?"

A wave of heat flushed through Laurel's body. *Park? Only your brother…*

"What's a DILF?"

"Dad I'd like to fu—"

Laurel slammed her hand over her friend's mouth. "April! That niece is here and can likely hear you."

April flung herself onto the couch and rolled her eyes. "Right."

"Have you seen how small this place is?"

April nodded. "Speaking of that… Where does my brother have you sleeping? And don't tell me you're sleeping in his room because that is just *eww*."

Laurel shook her head and patted the purple couch. "You're sitting on it."

"He put you on the *couch*?" The utter horror in April's expression made Laurel laugh. Her friend loved her expensive mattresses and high thread count sheets. The two of them were so different, yet those differences had never gotten in the way of them becoming so close.

"The only other option," Laurel explained, joining her friend on the couch, "would be to share a room with Shae, but, I don't know, I guess your brother wasn't comfortable with that. The couch isn't so bad. It pulls out."

April grinned and nodded as if she completely understood, at the same time smoothing a piece of hair between her fingertips. "At least tell me he's not being a total ass to you. Still a scary sex god?"

Sex god? Most definitely. Scary? Maybe not so much—that was, if she didn't count the fact that Micah's job was illegal, and risky, and put him and his family in danger. She still didn't know exactly what it was he did, but she had an idea it involved some sort of gang or crime family. The thought didn't sit well with her, especially that first night after he'd told her. Lying in the dark in the middle of his living room, shadows and flickers of light creeping along the carpet. Would *they*—the people who had Micah under their thumb—come to his home? Break in?

Quitting the job and leaving this part of the city had crossed her mind that night. She didn't want anything to do with whoever Micah was working for. But then she'd thought of the little six-year-old living in the apartment too. If Laurel left, that would mean Shae would go back to spending her days, and nights, in The Alibi's office. Her heart broke at the thought.

As for being an ass…Micah's temper had ebbed somewhat from when she'd first moved in. Like this morning, when she'd been getting Shae ready for school…

Laurel's fingers had quickly worked through Shae's hair. Only five more minutes until they'd needed to leave for the bus stop.

"You're making me look bad," Micah had said, his voice rough, though when she met his gaze in the mirror, there'd been something teasing about it.

Laurel's hand had frozen. "Bad?"

He'd stepped closer and pointed to the inside-out braid she was almost finished with. "All these fancy hair designs? People at school know I'm a single dad."

"Well." Laurel had grinned, partly because she was pleased with her creation, but mostly because he was giving her a compliment. "Maybe Mr. Single Dad took some hairstyling lessons."

His eyes had zeroed in on hers. "Or maybe…his daughter's nanny showed him a few tricks."

Hot, it had suddenly become hot in there. Not to mention extremely cramped.

"Yeah," Laurel had said quietly. "I could do that —"

A horn blared outside and Laurel blinked, April's face shrinking into focus. "He's warming up to me," Laurel told her friend.

April's perfectly groomed eyebrow lifted. "I told you he would. Though I have to admit, I wasn't expecting it to be after only a week. You must've made some impression on him."

Letting him strip her bare and pleasure her until she thrashed against him? Not exactly the impression she'd been hoping for. Nonetheless, trading that night for something more proper simply wasn't in the books. Her mind was like a greedy troll, hoarding every detail of the memory.

"He mentioned the other day," Laurel said, tucking her feet beneath her legs, "that he doesn't have a relationship with your dad anymore." Laurel had never spoken with April about her father, but since Micah's admission at the park — his father being the "rough one" — she wanted to know more.

April nodded, understanding softening her expression. "When Shae came into his life, he made a promise to himself that he wouldn't let his daughter be raised in the same environment we had."

"Which was…?" Laurel couldn't imagine worse than what she'd first walked in to — a six-year-old being raised in a bar, witness to drugs and alcohol, and now a father who she knew beat the crap out of criminals for money.

"A father who was a drunk," April explained. "Who spent every dollar he had and every waking moment fraternizing in a bar, getting in fights…"

Sounded a lot like Micah. "Your brother kept Shae in a bar. And he drinks beer."

April shook her head. "Shae was only there because he had no other option. And sure he drinks, but have you noticed he never has more than two?"

No, she hadn't noticed that.

There was the fighting, too, but Laurel told Micah she wouldn't say anything about it, so she asked, "Your father's still here in Boston then?" A strange part of her hoped he wasn't. She didn't want to think Micah had to deal with that too.

"No, he took off upstate when I was fifteen. Micah was nineteen. I honestly don't know where he is now."

Laurel scanned her friend, her well-put-together ensemble and lack of any sort of temper. "You don't seem fazed by it all," she mused, but as the words came out, the realization that April's obsession for materialistic things may have stemmed from a childhood of having nothing. The fact that she didn't want anything to do with kids likely a result of not growing up with a positive role model. Even a half-assed role model.

"Compared to my brother?" April nodded. "Not that our childhoods were all that different, but my dad was really hard on Micah."

"How so?"

"He was the oldest, and the only boy. My dad—asshole as he could be—would've never hit a girl. He wasn't abusive in *that* way."

"But he hit Micah?" Laurel's chest tightened. She hardly knew the man, but the thought of anyone going through that as a child shredded her insides.

"Everything was Micah's fault, if you get my drift."

It all made sense to Laurel—the closed-off way Micah was around her at times, the protective bubble he kept Shae in. He didn't want to be the father he'd had.

"Auntie April!" Shae screeched as she ran into the room. "Are you going to the movies with us?"

April ruffled the top of Shae's head. "What're you seeing, monkey face?"

"Queen's Heart."

April looked discreetly at Laurel, her nose scrunched, and mouthed, "A kiddie movie?"

Laurel shrugged. *What would you expect?* she said back with her eyes.

"I'm afraid I have an appointment I can't get out of, kid. But I'll catch you on the flipside."

Shae's shoulders hunched forward. "Okay." She took Laurel's hand. "Daddy said he has to work, but he wants to meet us there. He said to save a seat between us."

Between? That meant she'd have to spend an hour and a half in the dark, thinking about how close Micah's hands were to her body.

April nudged Laurel's leg with her foot and grinned suspiciously. "Impression," she sang quietly.

Popcorn, Milk Duds, and sodas in hand, the three of them—Shae, Micah, with Laurel on the end—reclined into the theater seats. She was inches from Micah but could still smell him—the musky scent that drew up image after image of his face between her legs.

Dear lord, this is going to be a long movie.

Micah hadn't had to work long—a quick errand he'd told her as he'd rushed out of his apartment earlier. By the time she and Shae were settling mid-theater in the row's center, he'd shown up with a drink of his own in hand. Laurel hadn't questioned the reddened welts strung across his knuckles aloud—she would never in front of Shae. She did, however, let him see her eyes lingering on them.

"Let's move to the edge," had been his only response.

"But the middle has a much better view," Laurel protested once she was sitting at the end of the row, propping her popcorn on her knees.

"It's also the hardest to get out of when the row is filled with people," Micah spouted back, his tone firm. "Which means longer to reach an exit should we need to."

Laurel craned her neck forward, trying not to stare at Micah's enormously muscled arms, and smiled at Shae. "Next time we won't bring you know who, and we'll sit in the middle. Deal?"

Shae nodded at the same time a large hand landed in Laurel's popcorn. "No deal," Micah said, pilfering a handful.

She looked over at him, meeting the chocolate brown eyes staring at her and teased, "Because you realize I'm right and you've actually been enjoying these family outings and don't want to miss another?"

"Because…" He drew closer, flicking his gaze at her mouth and his tongue across his. A colony of ants suddenly came to life in her stomach, scrambling frantically with the thought of his lips on hers. That tongue in her mouth. *Christ, am I ever going to be able to be near him and* not *think of my boss pleasuring me senseless?* No, he wouldn't kiss her here, in a theater surrounded with families and kids and *his daughter.* Clearly, however, he was relishing the warning of it. "Someone's got to have street smarts in the group."

Laurel frowned playfully. "Are you implying I don't?"

Suddenly, he was in her face, his arm like a bar across her body to the other side of her seat. "Seeing that you hung your purse on the aisle side of your chair, with easy access to anyone walking up the stairway"—he unslung the strap from the back and tucked the purse beneath her feet, his face not moving an inch—"I'd say *no.*"

"We're in a theater full of kids," she challenged back. "I doubt a princess-loving little kid is going to have their way with my belongings."

His eyes narrowed, and his lips moved closer to her ear. "Trust no one."

"I trust you," she whispered, immediately growing hot in the face. Why had she said that? And why could she not think straight when his mouth was anywhere near hers? His body loomed over her, pinning her into the cushy theater chair. For a fleeting moment, she wondered what it would feel like to be under him, stretched out on a bed with his massive arms propped on either side of her—

"I'm no longer a scary sex god?" he asked quietly with one of his rare and treasured smiles.

What? How did he—?

Hand flattened over his chest, she pushed him back and stared at him, horrified. "Your sister?"

"April may be tenacious, but I'm still her big brother. And

I can get anything out of her." Just then the lights dimmed and the movie screen lit with the start of the previews.

Anything? What else had her friend told him? Her lack of hookups in the last year? Lack of boyfriends too? Yeah, that wasn't something she wanted him knowing about.

Thoughts of Micah carried her through the first half of the movie. Seventeenth-century prince and princess. Joker sidekick. It was all very typical and allowed her mind to wander. If Micah knew it'd been a while since she'd been with anyone, what did he think after she'd given herself up so easily on his kitchen counter? Did he care at all?

Toward the end of the movie, Micah leaned across the armrest and whispered into Laurel's ear, "So the prince thinks he can win over the princess by proposing in front of the whole town? Seems a little cheesy, if you ask me."

"A town proposal is the ultimate way to win a lady's heart. It's romantic," she said without thinking, then nudged his chest with her elbow and teased, "Besides, no one asked you." His face hovered only inches from hers, lips in kissing distance should she incline to the side just a tad—

Darn her overcharged mind.

And *darn* his irresistibly sexy voice. It had her thinking dirty thoughts even while surrounded by packs of families and kids.

He crept closer. The brush of his hair against her face, accompanied by the warm sweep of heat from his skin, ignited her nerve endings in a mouthwatering, *I want to jump on top of you right here, right now* way.

Unexpectedly, his hand clutched around the opposite side of her head and turned her to face him. In the dim glow of the movie screen, his deep brown eyes looked murkier, almost black and predatory. It sent an actual shiver down her arms and legs.

"The prince has it all wrong," he said, his voice low and rough. "He doesn't need to impress the princess by embarrassing himself in front of the whole town." Micah paused. Licked his lips. *Darn those lips too!* "He needs to do something to make her feel *alive* and worth living for." His words and his breath... Was the room starting to spin?

"Like what?" she squeaked out.

"Take her someplace where the music is loud and the space is tight. Somewhere she can close her eyes and feel the beat of the music. Where he can put his hands here" — one massive hand landed on her hip. Fingers pressed into her backside. She sucked in a shaky breath — "and guide her body to move with his. To..." He edged closer, whispered in her ear, "rub against his."

She clamped her teeth over her lip, fighting the urge to press her mouth to his. With him this close, the scent of him had her heart pumping overtime. She inhaled slowly to suppress the compulsion and managed to say. "I doubt the seventeenth century had dance clubs."

"Well...they should've." And then his face was gone, and he was back in his seat with his eyes on the movie screen.

Holy mother of hot man in my face.

By the end of the movie, Laurel had no idea what had happened to the prince and princess — surely they must've ended up together. Instead, the image of Micah's hands on her hips, rubbing his body against hers kept her mind delectably occupied.

"So..." Micah said as the three of them made their way to the ice cream shop in the next block from the theater, "you really think you can spend all day, five days a week, babysitting a classroom full of whiny kids?" Not exactly the conversation he was going for, but he was desperately trying to rid his mind of the image he'd painted for Laurel during the movie. Her slim body glistening with sweat, her hips swaying and circling against his...

Yeah, talking about kids should do the trick.

She laughed. "They're not *all* whiny. Most, in fact, are better behaved at school than at home."

"They tell you that in teacher school?" he teased and slid his hand over her shoulder to guide her around the trio of forty-something guys approaching from the opposite direction. Dressed in business suits, they'd all three run their slimy gazes over Laurel, and the sight burned Micah's chest. Jealous? No, he couldn't have been. She was nothing but his temporary back scratcher. One he wanted to scratch all over his—

Jesus, man. You're acting hornier than a rabid fifteen-year-old.

Laurel stiffened under the weight of his arm, her shoulders rolling back as she glanced up to meet his eyes. Was she scared of him because of what he'd told her about his side job? Worried about his touch because technically he was her boss? Or uncomfortable because he was her best friend's older brother? "Not school," she said, her hand twitching against her side as if she'd thought to take his hand but instead thought better of it. "Growing up in a house with both parents as teachers, it's pretty much all I heard whenever I caused trouble."

He raised a brow and laughed. "You, cause trouble? That would be as believable as my sister shopping at Goodwill."

Even under the yellow glow of the afternoon sun, her face flushed red. A naughty side to his sweet, reserved nanny? And there went the control he'd just gained over the swelling in his pants.

"What about you?" she asked quickly, obviously in an attempt to flip the focus off her. He wanted to know more, to ask what kind of trouble she'd gotten into. What kind of childhood she'd had, and what it was like to have two normal parents who'd loved and raised her with the best of intentions. Anyone with teachers as parents and the hope of teaching kids in her future had to have been raised with all that, right?

Squinting against the sun, she smiled at him. Up ahead, Shae stooped to pick a ladybug off an overgrown rose bush. "I'm curious how you were in school," she added.

Troublemaker.

Unruly and disruptive.

What other names had he heard teachers call him back then?

"Just be glad," he said, drawing her in tighter against him, "as a future teacher, I'm well past my childhood."

Laurel wrinkled her nose. "That bad?"

"I was pretty uncontrollable." To put it nicely.

"What's the worst thing you did?"

At which school? Over the years, he'd been moved from school to school because of his behavior. "Mostly fights," he said, peering down to gauge her reaction. He wasn't that person anymore—with zero ruling over his temper. He still fought, but those parameters were set, he liked to think, and he was in much more control. "But there was this one time in high school I pissed off the principal pretty bad."

Laurel's head jerked back. "Uh oh. What'd you do?"

"Other than being disruptive, disrespectful, defiant, and disobedient toward staff at all times?" He chuckled lightly. Christ, he'd been such an asshole student back then. "One time in history, the teacher failed me for having too many absences. So, *naturally*, I made a sculpture out of textbooks in the classroom and then called the teacher a philistine for knocking it down."

"Oh my god." She giggled. "During class?"

He nodded. "Security brought me to the principal, and instead of just 'fessing up and complying with my detention sentence, I repeatedly answered his questions about why I did it with smartass remarks."

"Like?"

"Like…" Geez, he hadn't thought about those years in ages. What was it he'd said to Principal Buckskin? "'I can't tell you why I stole the key to the book cabinet, as it would go against my religion to prove the existence of the holy motherfucker upstairs.'"

Her hand slapped over her mouth, and she laughed louder. "You didn't!"

He cringed. "I did."

"What did your parents say?"

Parents.

Father.

Fuck, why had he led the conversation there? His stomach churned, legs grew restless. He drew back his arm and slowed his steps, all too aware of the way Laurel was looking at him. Her searching eyes and the divot materializing between them.

If he gave her this, would she stop prying? Stop trying to know about that part he was trying to forget?

"It was just my dad," he said lowly, stiffening his muscles so she wouldn't feel him flinch. "And he literally beat the shit out of me. Said if I was going to get kicked out of school, it'd better be for fighting and not messing with the principal's head."

Laurel's hand rested on his arm and she spun, at the same time tugging him to a stop. And it wasn't until she smoothed her fingers gently over his forehead and down his jaw that he realized he'd been gritting his teeth. Talk of his father always seemed to do that.

"Why would he want you to fight?" she asked, her voice soft, a strange blend of curiosity and concern.

Micah shrugged, swallowing against the pressure building in his chest. God, how he hated with a passion talking about that part of his life. "Boozing and brawling," he ground out. "It was his way of life."

Short and sweet. No further explanation needed.

A moment of silence fell between them, Laurel's eyes and fingertips scanning every inch of his face. The inspection unnerved him, but it was nothing compared to the way his world jolted to the side when she stood on her tiptoes, whispered, "I'm so sorry," and pressed a gentle kiss to his lips.

Chapter Nine

"You want the good or bad news first?" Ryan said, slamming a stack of paper folders onto the bar next to where Micah picked at the remains of his burger and fries. If he'd had the choice, he'd have gone home for dinner—Laurel's home cooking was far better than fast food—but there was too much to do if he was going to be taking off early again tonight.

"Considering you just met with Jackson and we desperately need that Bud account to continue, I'll take the good."

Ryan lowered onto the stool next to him and snatched a fry, shoving it into his mouth. A piece of the innards clung to his bushy beard, and Micah just shook his head. How long was Ryan going to keep growing that thing? It had been a bet more than six months ago that he wouldn't be able to handle it, and Ryan hadn't picked up a razor since. "Well, because we've been with his company for a year now, we've got a track record. And as I've been in charge of the ordering, that track record is virtually spotless."

"*Virtually?*"

Ryan shrugged and stole another fry. "There may have been one mishap."

"Showing up to the cock-fight-slash-meeting with a six-year-old you were supposed to be babysitting?" Micah teased and shoved the unfolded wrapper with his leftovers Ryan's way. Fucking Ryan and his insane ideas...

A lightness bloomed in Micah's chest knowing he had Laurel to watch Shae now. Someone with a heart of gold and the intentions of a nun—when it came to kids at least.

"No, that meeting proved we had a solid relationship with our supplier, thank you very much. Anyway"—he averted his eyes to the food, which Micah knew was his way of hiding something—"they're willing to give us a more attractive pricing and better payment terms—no more cash only—so we can invest less capital in the inventory."

No more cash only; that was good news. "All right, so what's the bad news?"

Ryan finished off the fries and crumpled the wrapper. "He said we're already acting like old bar owners, getting comfortable with our regular customers, that we're missing the opportunity with new customers." He twisted on the stool, throwing his feet onto the ground. "They're our next meal ticket. The only way to keep a neighborhood pub in business."

Micah lifted a brow. "What does he want us to do? Lure in uppity subbies with the promise of a cold Bud and some fancy projector screen playing black-and-white movies? Have you seen the neighborhood we're in?"

"No black and whites," Ryan said, shaking his head. "I

was thinking something a little *less* classy."

"Like?" Jesus, what did his friend have in mind? If it was anything like his ideas back when they were kids, Micah knew he was in for a shit show.

"Turn this place into a night club on Saturdays. Hire a DJ, clear the tables in the middle for a dance floor, get one of those ridiculous globe lights to hang up." Ryan grinned. "It could make us a lot of money, bringing in the crowds like that."

"If anyone showed up…"

"They would if we promoted it right."

Just then the door to the bar creaked open, silhouetting a slim body in the evening sun. A woman, obviously, with long hair flowing over her bare shoulders. Both Ryan and Micah squinted into the brightness flooding the room, dust motes drifting over the empty tables.

"Tell me," Ryan spouted to the woman, "would you be more interested in this place if you could get a little bump-and-grind action? Meet some nice guys? Maybe go home with one?"

The woman giggled and swung the door wider. A mini silhouette popped into the room. "Bump and grind? Uncle Ryan, you have a tractor? I've always wanted to ride one!"

Fuck. Shae.

Micah punched Ryan's arm and stood. "You talk to everyone's nanny that way?" Then he looked to Laurel, who he could see now that the door was closed and the sun wasn't blinding him. Tight jeans and an even tighter T-shirt, looking casually adorable and *nothing* like the type of girls who would be found bumping and grinding in a bar. "My friend evidently missed the manners train growing up."

Laurel smiled brightly, not thrown one bit by Ryan's inappropriate interrogation. "Sounds like your sister."

"Sorry," Ryan rushed out, clearing the trash from the bar. "Didn't realize you were someone Micah knew."

"It's okay," Laurel said, adjusting the small purse strap across her chest. The leather band fit between her breasts, pushing in the thin cotton material. An unspoiled view to what lay beneath. "At least you didn't hit me with an inappropriate pick-up line. That might have been awkward."

Ryan nodded, his eyes caressing the show Laurel's purse strap was putting on, and a stab of something hot pierced through Micah's chest. Quickly, he reached for the purse. "Let me take that for you."

"Thanks. Am I staying?" She held up a small square of paper—the note Micah had left on the counter in the apartment earlier that morning: *Meet me at The Alibi at 5:00. Bring Shae.* He wasn't sure what he was doing; he only knew these tickets had fallen into his lap, and the thought of taking anyone other than Laurel and Shae repelled him.

"Actually, no." He tucked the purse under his arm, not paying attention at all to the scrutiny he could feel Ryan giving him. "The game starts in an hour, but it'll take a little while to get there. Especially with commuter traffic."

"Game?" All three of them—Ryan, Shae, and his delectable nanny—said at once.

"Dude," Ryan spouted. "You're taking off? Again? Just when we were about to plan an event for this weekend?"

Shae tugged on his hand. "What kind of game, Daddy?"

"Off-season hockey training," he told her then looked at Ryan. "Free tickets. You wouldn't have passed them up, either. I'll be in tomorrow to help you plan your stupid *bump-and-grind* experience."

"Experience?" Ryan smiled and punched Micah's arm. "That's it! It's going to be an experience. *The* Experience. Something people will never forget. Something that'll keep bringing 'em back." He started for the back office. "I'll work on the flyers. Tomorrow you can team up with Trey to build a new drink list."

Micah shrugged. Whatever his friend wanted…

Laurel glanced up at him, her head tilted to the side, and frowned. "Hockey game? Aren't those freezing inside?" She pinched the hem of her thin T-shirt and stretched it out. "There's a sweater in the car for Shae, but I don't have anything warmer than this."

Why hadn't he thought of that? And how hard would it have been to add to the note: *dress warm*? Micah glanced to his long-sleeved shirt—not exactly something he could offer her—when he suddenly remembered. "I've got an extra sweatshirt back in my office."

B ig, black, and bulky with the words THE ALIBI written in blood red across the chest. And Lord did it smell like Micah. The spicy scent that set her nerves aflame every time she smelled it.

Discreetly, Laurel lowered her nose to the material and inhaled. Masochistic, she knew. She couldn't have her boss—*again*—without the risk of him coming to his senses and firing her for inappropriate work behavior, and yet she couldn't stop drowning herself in his scent. Couldn't stop imagining what it would be like if she did. Her hands on him, his on her. All over and searching to give her a beyond-belief orgas—

Another body hit the Plexiglas in front of them, and Laurel jumped with a screech. "Jesus, do the players have to keep doing that?"

Micah and Shae, sitting on the freezing-cold bench beside her, laughed. "I take it this is your first hockey game?"

The crowd cheered. Micah grinned. Yeah, that gorgeous smile was doing nothing to help get rid of the absurd thoughts about him. She nodded, feeling her cheeks warm with the admission, "I've watched one on TV once."

He patted her knee and said to his daughter, "Looks like we need to get Laurel out more often."

Two more players rammed the clear barrier and then started to fight. Armed with sticks in their hands, they pushed and shoved and swung their arms until a referee skated over to break them up. Roars from the spectators grew louder, barking the words, "Fight! Fight! Fight!"

Laurel held very still, noticing Micah's hand hadn't yet moved from her leg. Close to her knee, but enough pressure to feel the heat from it seeping through her jeans. *Move your hand up my leg, Micah. No, don't move your hand up my leg. Jeez, why am I thinking about him moving his hand up my leg?* She pointed to the ice. "Do they always fight like that?"

"Those are the enforcers. Or goons. And fighting in hockey is part of the code. Officials permit it, one, because they say it helps deter other types of rough play and allows teams to protect their star players, and, two, because it's a considerable draw for the sport. Fans love it."

Including his six-year-old, she thought as she noticed Shae's undivided attention on the players separating from the fight.

Micah narrowed his stare on her. "You're judging me for bringing her here, aren't you?"

She was, but her intentions weren't to make him feel bad about it. "I just think there might be *less violent* sports that would be better for her to watch."

Suddenly, Shae leaned across her dad, cocked her head to the side, and said bluntly, "Fighting is bad. Daddy told me that after we went to watch the chickens fight."

Chickens fight? "You mean—"

"Not me," Micah spouted quickly. "Ryan. And I already told him what a shithead he was for taking her."

Laurel scolded him with her eyes for cussing in front of Shae, then absently nodded. All this fighting... It brought up the memory of what he'd told her about his other job. Fighting people to pay money.

Carefully, she leaned closer to him and whispered, "Don't you worry that you'll run into the wrong kind of people when you're...working?"

Through the material of his shirt, his arm muscles stiffened. "People like...?"

"Them." She pointed to a group of men at the curve of the stadium. Sitting front row like her and her companions, but looking more out of place than anyone else with their black leather jackets and cigarettes tucked behind their ears. Tattoos littered their necks and shaved scalps and... "Dangerous people?" Even she could hear the tightness in her voice.

Was she worried about him? Did she care enough about him to even *be* worried?

The constricting in her chest answered that question

for her. She swallowed against it and added, "It just seems so risky. Jumping into something with someone you know nothing about." She lowered her voice and peeked at Shae to make sure she didn't have prying ears. "How do you know the people don't have...*guns*?"

Their eyes met. His didn't move an inch. "I don't," was all he said, but with a punch of finality. Boozing and brawling— it was what he'd said his father did. And while Micah wasn't a drunk like April had said their father was, the tendency to fight might have had something to do with the way he'd been raised. The thought sent an achy wave outward from her heart, all the way to the top of her head and the tips of her toes.

"You don't have to do it, you know. Work with those people? I'm sure there are other ways to make money."

"Says the girl who couldn't find a real summer job and is instead babysitting for her best friend's brother." He rolled his eyes. "The money pays for Shae's school and your salary and I can't afford to lose either right now. Besides, I already told you I don't have a choice. I'm stuck."

Or...it was all he knew. Was what he was comfortable doing. Easy fight; easy money. *Psychology 101, Laurel.* That same feeling when she saw a child in need of help hit her. Hard. Micah was no different. And she wanted desperately to fix him.

Micah pulled the covers over Shae's sleeping body and tucked in the edges of the blanket. Laurel, standing in the doorway of the dark room, didn't feel like she was required for the bedtime routine but couldn't pull herself from the doorway either. Micah was trying with Shae, given his circumstances, and that was the difference between him and most men who were raised in ugly conditions like his.

She stepped back as he exited then quietly shut the door.

"Long night." A thin smile stretched his lips. "Are you tired?"

"No." She returned his smile, stepping into his space. Just an inch, but enough to hint to what she might be up to. She tilted her head up. "I was thinking a glass of wine. Want to join me?"

His eyes caressed her from head to toe. She'd since removed the bar sweatshirt, and the sight of Micah's eyes on her chest had her nipples hardening instantly. "Yeah," he said lowly, "a nightcap would be good."

Oh, she was thinking more than a nightcap, but if she told him her plan, he may not want to stay up with her. Then again, he was a guy, and guys liked to—

"Great," she spouted. "I'll get the drinks."

In the kitchen, she tucked a bottle of white wine under her arm and grabbed the corkscrew along with two glasses then headed to the purple couch. Sitting directly in the middle with his legs planted in front of him, Micah watched as she set the wine and glasses on the small end table, uncorked the bottle, and poured.

The couch wasn't huge, but there was room on either side of him. She handed him a glass, stole a bottomless breath of confidence, and instead climbed on top of him, straddling her legs on the sides of his. Jeans on jeans, though her body suddenly ignited. "This okay?" she asked in the most seductive tone she could muster. Inside she laughed. Since when had she become a seductress?

That answer was easy. Since she'd known what it was like to kiss Micah. To feel his hands, his lips, his tongue on her. *In* her.

The buzzing of her insides kicked into overdrive when he stilled for a moment, that intense, stony gaze devouring her. Assessing her. Then, slowly, his hand ran up her leg and rested at the curve of her waist, and he smiled.

He.

Smiled.

And it was beautiful and breathtaking, and every cell in her body wished he would do that more often.

Then he lifted a brow. "I don't know any guy who would turn down a gorgeous girl on his lap." He took a swig of his wine then set the glass on the table. "Is that all you plan to do?" Beneath the swoop of brown hair across his forehead, his eyes pierced her with a wolf-like intensity.

That look…it filled and deflated her at the same time. She wanted him, wanted to explore this dangerous, daring feeling that consumed her when she was near him. But the more conscientious side of her brain wondered if and when Micah was going to come to his senses and let her go, because *this* wasn't what he'd hired her for.

"Only if you want it to be," she said anyway, running a hand up his arm and under the sleeve of his shirt. Her fingertips bumped over the definition in his arm—the swell of his muscles and divots in between. "I *am* technically your employee, you know."

"You also live in my apartment. Sort of a fine line if you ask me." He took the glass out of her hand and joined it with his. Then he waited.

"I apologize for bringing up your job tonight." It wasn't something she'd planned on saying. But sitting there, face to face with him and feeling the openness blossoming between them, it'd just sort of slipped out. The beat of her heart at the base of her throat shook her voice when she added, "I just—"

"You feel sorry for me." His hands twitched at her sides—the only sign of his irritation.

Quickly, she shook her head. "Not sorry…" How did she explain it without sounding too maternal? Without telling him she simply wanted to make him forget about all that for a moment? "I talked to April the other day," she said, smoothing her finger over the crease growing across his forehead. "Not about your work, but she told me about your father. The way you two were raised. And I get that you had a difficult childhood, but that childhood—and those struggles you went through—made you who you are." Curling in her fingers, she traced a line across the angles of his jaw with the backs of her knuckles. "And…I don't know, I like the way you are."

He reached up and touched the gold chain around her neck. "Even though I'm big and scary?" The teasing air to his words didn't match the intensity of his gaze, and the contradiction between the two knocked her head into a bobbling wave for a splinter of a second.

She pulled her other hand out from his sleeve and ran it down his chest. Lower and lower until it was hovering over the button of his jeans. "Not all of you is scary."

Quietly they stared at each other, until she slowly dipped her head and without waiting for permission pressed a long kiss to his lips. She placed soft kisses all over his mouth until the kisses became longer and more intense. His tongue eventually parted her lips, and the taste of sweet wine blasted her senses, the teasing vanishing along with her mind.

His hands started to move over her body—up her back, around her waist, cupping her breasts, one and then the other. The kiss grew into a charged detonation that, along with the searching of his tongue in her mouth and hands that wouldn't sit still on her body, had her wondering if she'd ever be able to find her breath.

Tightening his arms around her, he stood, and without breaking the kiss, walked them down the hallway and into his bedroom. The door shut. He nibbled her lip and lowered to the edge of his bed, straddling her legs over his middle in the same position they were in before.

She planted her hands on his shoulders and pushed back, stealing a moment to look around his room.

Micah pinched the tip of her chin between his fingers and tipped her face so she was looking directly at him. "This is my room," he said, his jaw set, but not with anger. "And I'll only give you five seconds to take it in before I put my mouth back on yours."

She giggled. "Are you trying to be scary now?" But her eyes were already skipping over the room. Gray walls, a dresser, TV, and several pictures of Shae, nothing that gave her anything more than what she previously knew—

Lips crashed into hers, Micah's hand secured around her head, and then they were kissing. Fast. And hard. And *oh my gosh I can't breathe again.*

Breathless, she broke the kiss and slid off his legs. To the floor. On her knees. Directly in front of him. His brown eyes locked with hers—narrowed and penetrating. Christ, had she ever felt this vulnerable and powerful at the same time?

In her gut, she knew the answer was no. She'd never been with a man who gave her the commanding ability to unabashedly pop the button on his jeans and slide down the zipper.

A low growl echoed from Micah's chest as she freed his erection from the material and ran her tongue in a long, slow line from the top to the bottom.

"Oh, fuck, Laurel." He reached for her, but she intercepted, tucking his hands beneath the sides of his legs.

"No touching." A devilish smile lifted the corners of her mouth. "Can you do that, Micah Crane? Not be the big, tough, scary guy running the show?" Another swipe of her tongue on him, and he slammed his head back in response.

He grit out through his teeth, "Didn't you just say I wasn't scary?"

She wrapped her hand at the base of his erection and perched just above the head, her breath whispering against his skin. "Not all of you. Besides, you don't have me fooled. I know there's a heart of gold somewhere in you." And then she swallowed his cock into her mouth.

He couldn't breathe. He couldn't talk. And because of this little seductress of his, he couldn't fucking touch her either.

Shit, not that he was complaining. A hot blonde sliding her lips up and down him? Licking and sucking to send tiny ripples of pleasure throughout his entire core?

Had he died and gone to fucking heaven?

No, he hadn't. Because when she slid her lips to the head of his cock and hummed lowly, a spine-tingling tremor rocked his body clear down to his toes. Still pinned beneath his legs, his hands itched to wrap around her head, guide her to repeat that move over and over again until he exploded.

He wanted to drown in the feel of her. Bury himself in her sweet-tasting pussy. Lie with her on top of him, riding his cock into goddamn oblivion—

Vibrations paralyzed his thoughts, his every muscle, and the sound of Laurel humming became his new favorite sound. He threw back his head and closed his eyes, clenching his entire body against the warm fingers now cupping and cradling and handling his balls.

"Jesus, Laurel. Who the hell taught you to do this?"

A giggle and a tiny nip to his inner thigh was all he got in response. And then her mouth was back on him, moving up and down, sucking hard and then soft, until he felt the pressure build from deep in his core.

He lifted his leg to remove his hand and no sooner did hers slam down on top of it. "One rule, Micah. Did you forget it so soon?" Her tongue lapped up his shaft, and he drew in a shallow breath then narrowed his stare on hers.

"I'm going to come if you keep doing that."

Glassy and blown to the edges, her eyes searched his. "Isn't that the point?" Before he could respond, her lips circled him and sank clear down to the base. She withdrew in a painfully long stroke then repeated.

And repeated.

And repeated.

"Okay," he grit out, tightening to withstand—*and slow*—the soul-crushing force about to explode from him.

"You don't need to—"

"Stop talking, Micah..." Her tongue flicked his head, and that devilish smile returned. One hand gripped his balls, the other the base of his dick, and she said, "And come in my mouth."

Well, shit, if that wasn't the hottest thing he'd ever heard a woman say. But was she sure? She didn't really seem like the type—

The humming started again, high-pitched and right at the head. Damn to all hell the stereotypes of this woman— obviously she had a wilder side than she'd let on. The thought of finding it, of discovering what else she could do with that amazing body, sent dirty, porn-like images flashing through his head until he couldn't resist the pressure anymore.

He groaned, and release came, and when he finally opened his eyes, Laurel was licking her glistening lips. Damn, she was beautiful with her long hair draped in waves over her shoulders and ocean-blue eyes heavy-lidded and sated. She pursed her lips into a sexy smile and started to stand.

But Micah wasn't done. He wanted more of her. "Come here," he said, quickly dislodging his hands and wrapping them around her head. He leaned closer, his mouth poised over hers when she reared back with a crinkled brow and cleared her throat.

"Isn't it general rule that guys don't kiss after...um... *that*."

Inside, he smiled. So he was right. The seductress act was purely that—an act. "Only guys who have zero respect for women don't." He closed the space and took her mouth completely, stroking his tongue against her lips until they parted.

The kiss was slow. Gentle. And like something two people in love would share. The thought snapped against his brain like a live wire, jolting him away from her.

No, there weren't any feelings involved here. Laurel was just a girl he could conveniently get his hands on.

"You never answered my question," he said in an attempt to cover up the way he'd torn away from her so quickly. He slid his thumb in a soft line across her mouth. "Your technique…is that something you read in a magazine?"

Her eyes glinted. "No magazine."

He cocked his head, nodding away the word his brain threw at him: *experience*. "A friend, then?"

Not jealous, he told himself, if her experience had been how she'd gotten those skills. Just curiosity.

Unexpectedly, Laurel wrapped her mouth around his thumb and sucked it from bottom to top. Then she grinned and answered, "Yep. Your sister."

Chapter Ten

"Stripper poles and a Fireball waterfall."

Micah blinked, the memory of Laurel's lips wrapped around him disappearing faster than he could say, "What the hell?"

Ryan laughed and sucker-punched his shoulder. "Seriously? I've been talking to you for a good five minutes, and all I've gotten is a weak nod from you and an even weaker 'Mmm-hmm.'"

Because he hadn't wanted to let that memory of Laurel go. And, damn it, he just had.

Micah leaned back in his desk chair and ran his hand through his hair. At least his lower half was hidden behind the desk. "You can't put a fucking stripper pole in here."

The flyer from Ryan's hand fluttered to the desktop in front of him. "Don't worry, we're keeping The Experience as classy as The Alibi. Midori Sours and Lemon Drop shots to bring in the ladies, dollar beers for the guys, and the best

DJ in town. You should tell that cute little nanny of yours. I'm sure she's looking to meet someone to take away her innocence for a night." He smiled wryly. "A little bump-and-grind action? Top it off with a one-night—"

"Shut the hell up, Ryan." Micah shoved out of his chair and forced an uncaring smile—one that warred against the hot rush pulsing in his chest.

"Ha!" Ryan's hand whacked the wooden desk, the sound echoing in the tiny office. "I knew it."

Micah scowled. "Knew what?"

"That you like her. The nanny."

"Of course I like her. I hired her to watch over my daughter."

Ryan shook his head. "I mean you have the hots for her. You like-like her. You have a crush on her."

"And did we suddenly become twelve again?" Micah folded his arms over his front side, the piercing heat spreading to his neck and shoulders. "Grown men don't get *crushes*. And they definitely don't *like-like* people."

"Call it what you want, but I saw it last night. You smiled at her. And you don't ever fucking smile." He shrugged and picked up the flyer. "It's no big deal, man. A relationship with a nanny? It might do wonders to wipe some of the asshole off you." The teasing manner to the words had Micah's fists clenching hard, but Ryan—being the dick he was—didn't stop there. He faced Micah and rattled the piece of paper. "I'd say it's working already. You do realize you've been here for four hours and have yet to slam a door? Whatever you're feeling for her…" He winked then chuckled. "Keep it up. Less tension bottled inside my partner makes for a much easier day in the office."

Micah stiffened. Feeling for her? There weren't any feelings involved in his little escapades with Laurel. Were there?

A couple nights to let shit go… That was all they'd had.

Ryan added, "In fact, maybe you should tell her."

Yeah, that was enough; he didn't have to sit around and take this shit from his partner. "Nice theory, jackass," he spat out and headed for the door. "But I think all that hair on your face is messing with your ability to think straight."

Ryan laughed. "You call it a beard. I call it awesomeness escaping through my face. Potato, po-*tah*-to."

The door slammed and Ryan's annoying-as-hell chuckle faded into the distance. Outside, Micah dialed his phone. He'd show Ryan exactly what kind of feelings he'd been having for his little nanny.

"What about Shae? Who's going to watch her?" Laurel tilted her chin to better see Micah. Not that he was dressed any differently than he normally was with jeans and a T-shirt, but the way that black shirt clung to the rippled muscles beneath had her hands itching to run across his chest. Over his tattooed arm and down to his—

You really need to stop fantasizing about your boss.

If only she had a dollar for every time her common sense had to remind her of that over the last few days.

Micah stepped closer, the scent of his cologne momentarily dizzying her. "Mrs. Briggs, the old lady next door, is going to watch her."

"Old lady?"

Micah narrowed his eyes on her, the intensity of his gaze feeling like fire on her skin. Jesus, why did he do that to her? "She's not that old. Maybe sixty-five." His eyes looked her over. "Are you going to wear that or do you want time to change?"

A dance club. He was taking her to The Experience. She scanned her outfit: yoga pants and a tank with a cardigan. Unquestionably not appropriate for dancing.

She scrunched her nose. "Give me a few minutes to find something else?"

Twenty-five minutes later Laurel emerged from Micah's tiny apartment bathroom. She tugged the waist of her flowy cotton shorts higher and looked down at her simple tan wedges, thankful she'd packed at least one pair of heels. April was probably going to have a cow at the outfit Laurel had thrown together—diva as she was—but at least she couldn't say Laurel was being too modest with her choices. She'd made sure of that by folding over the elastic waist of the shorts to show off as much leg as possible.

Was it too much, seeing that she was going to the club with her boss?

Ha, not after the blowjob you gave him.

A low, drawn-out whistle filled the kitchen as she entered, a half-empty beer bottle perched at Micah's lips. Lips she suddenly couldn't take her eyes off. He smiled. "You look amazing."

Heat flushed over her entire body. "Thanks. I didn't exactly pack for a night at the club."

His gaze lingered on the crocheted hem of her flowery shorts. Was he a leg man? Did she even care if he was? She would've been lying to herself if she'd said no. Of course she cared. What else would explain the way her insides became jitterbugs when he was near? Why she'd mentally given herself a high five when she'd found out she would be spending the evening with him, sans his daughter. This was one night she could let loose, and she was not going to let it slip by her. She held up her small, plastic bra-strap clip. "Would you mind helping me? I can't ever get these on myself."

A wrinkle formed across his forehead. "You wear letter openers?"

She laughed and stepped closer to him. "It pulls my bra straps together so they won't show with this racer-back style tank." She smiled, remembering the first time April had introduced her to these nifty little devices.

God, April had said, *your bra straps stand out like ugly stretch marks. Come over here.* It had been their first week together as roommates. Quite the shellshock going from friends at school with April to living with her day in and day out. On the surface her best friend was blunt and irked by anything not at her speed. But Laurel had known her long enough to realize there was much more beneath April's shell than she let people see.

Micah's warm fingers slipping under the fabric on her shoulders drew her back to the kitchen. "How does this work exactly?" he said, at the same time caressing between her shoulder blades. Her skin suddenly felt like the victim of a cactus—all prickly and stinging, but penetrating to every single cell. Her body called to his. As if he knew she'd suddenly become putty in his hands, he dipped his thumb under one of the straps and ran it over her shoulder, causing the lacey material covering her breast to sag. Then his mouth was at her ear, his hard body pressed up against her backside. "Does it go like this?"

She inhaled a quick breath. Jesus, he felt so good. His hand plunged into the loosened cup and around her breast, taking it fully in his palm. He hadn't touched her like that since he'd had his way with her on the counter. The memory of his mouth between her legs, his tongue licking and swirling her into a lust coma, suddenly had her knees threatening to buckle.

His other hand swooped around her belly and pulled her closer, guiding her directly into his erection. "Or like this?"

Another weak breath. Was the room shrinking on her? The ceiling falling? Was she even standing anymore? She closed her eyes and imagined herself facedown on his bed, the weight of his body pinning her firmly into the mattress as he sank his—

On the counter, her phone buzzed. She reached for it, releasing a long, frustrated sigh but careful not to disrupt the connection his hand had with her boob.

"My sister and her impeccable timing," he whispered into her ear, eyeing the text message on her phone as she read it. *Leaving now.*

"Maybe I shouldn't have invited her."

"Or maybe," he said, reaching for the phone, "we could tell her to wait because her big brother would like to stick his—"

"No!" As fast as she could, she twirled and snatched the phone, laughing. "You wouldn't say that to her."

One dark eyebrow arched, and he cocked his head to

the side. "I wouldn't?"

"Not unless you want a swift ass kicking by the girl who knows Tae Kwon Do."

He chuckled. "My sister told you she knows Tae Kwon Do?"

Laurel shook her head. "Not me. A guy who was hitting on her in a bar a few months ago. I think her exact words were 'If you call me *sweetie* one more time, I'm going to Tae Kwon Do your ass until the only word you can say is douchebag.'"

"That's tactful."

"At least we don't ever have to worry about her being taken advantage of." Laurel quickly responded to April's text, telling her that they too were leaving, then tucked her phone into her purse. "Shall we go?"

The Alibi had been completely transformed with a dance floor in the center where tables and chairs usually sat, blue lights lining the bar's edge and wrapping up the existing pillars, and a disco ball that sent a kaleidoscope of colors along the floor. The place was packed with people, mostly college-aged kids, all standing belly up to the bar or lingering near pedestal tables along the room's edges. Music filled the space, but not one person was dancing.

"It's like a middle school dance gone bad," Micah said, clutching Laurel's hand. "Ryan's probably shitting his boxers right now. Let's go find him." He led her across the empty dance floor, the sound of her wedged heels on the glossy wood falling silent to the bump of the music.

In college she'd never much enjoyed the club scene—strangers rubbing their crotches and backsides up against her? Sweat mixing and hands groping? Laurel shook off a shiver. *At least I'm here with someone I know.*

And wouldn't mind if his hands did a little groping.

They found Ryan perched in the hallway near the bathroom, his fingers tapping vigorously on the screen of his phone, a divot the size of the Grand Canyon sprawled between his brows. "Motherfucking bathroom just took a shit." He pointed to the closed door of the men's restroom. "Something with the toilet, or the plumbing, or, fuck, I have no idea. Management's not answering, either. Don't they have someone who works after hours for this kind of thing?" His long beard, as he talked, held stiff.

"Did you try a plunger? Maybe it's just clogged."

"Bro, I tried a plunger, a tree branch… Whatever is in there is like a goddamn serpent." He hit send on the message he was typing and shoved his phone into his pocket. "This is so not the night for this." Then he looked at Laurel, like he'd just noticed she was standing there, then to the hand of hers that was entwined with Micah's. He smiled kindly at her and said, "Thanks for coming," before sliding his gaze to Micah. Funny, even with the thick, dark hair covering the entire bottom half of Ryan's face, she could still tell that when he directed his smile at Micah there was some sort of knowing to it. "Potato, po-*tah*-to," he said and laughed.

Micah stiffened and jerked his hand from Laurel's. "So what do you want us to do?"

Just then, April—dressed in a tight red skirt and flashy gold heels—exited the women's bathroom and squealed when she saw Laurel.

"Yay for dirty dancing nights at the bar!" Her vibrant smile warmed Laurel, and her arms encased her, squeezing tight. Really tight. Laurel eased back and poked the slender lines of toned muscles that stretched from her shoulder to elbow.

"Umm…Tae Kwon Do?" Laurel asked with a grin.

April's eyes brightened. "Nope. Crossfit. You'd never guess how good-looking the guys are in there. You should come with me sometime." For a moment, she scrunched her nose, the light smattering of freckles jumping together. "I doubt your scrawny arms would be able to lift a forty-five pound bar, but what better way to meet a guy?" She lifted her hand to her mouth, fingers outstretched like a prim and proper woman from the olden days. "Oh, dear, this pole is much too heavy—"

Micah cleared his throat, and April scowled at him.

"What's got your panties in a wad, big brother?" She reached out to poke his chest, and he swatted her hand away like a big brother would.

"Are you done playing fantasy over here?"

Laurel wasn't sure if the other two had heard it too, but there had unquestionably been a hint of irritation in those words. Because of the suggestion Laurel go out and meet other men? Did that mean he was jealous?

Why was she worrying about that anyway?

Ryan ran his hand down his beard. "Guess we'll just have a coed bathroom and hope no one has to unload a big one. Lisa's making me signs right now." He nodded over Laurel's shoulder to the dance floor. "Maybe you two could do something about that?"

Micah nodded, his features crinkled like he was thinking

hard about something. "What's wrong with the dance floor?"

"Well, fucker, this is a dance club, and it's totally vacant. The night is still young, which means this is the make-or-break moment when people either start dancing or start leaving. I just need someone to put the idea in their heads about which is the better choice."

"You want us to dance?"

"Unless you have another way to get people out there. Organize a chicken dance? A goddamn flash mob? I don't even care, but the dance floor needs its cherry popped, and it's not like people want to see me out there by myself."

"Ryan, you know I don't dance." Micah didn't sound angry, just simple and matter of fact, as if he were telling the time.

"Fine, then." Ryan reached for Laurel's hand. "You can stand watch to make sure no one goes in there and worsens this situation while I go show off my moves with your girlfriend."

"Um," Laurel sputtered at that last word at the same time Micah snatched her hand and tugged her away from Ryan.

"You're not going anywhere near her."

Ryan's eyes glinted and he stepped back. "Option number three is you dance with your sister."

"Eww," April said in a hurry, dragging the scooped neck of her black tank a little lower to show off the generous mounds God had graced her with. "Never happening." She winked at Ryan. "I'll dance with you, though. It'd be a good excuse to finally run my fingers through that beard."

Micah stiffened. "You're not dancing with him, either."

"Good." Ryan faced Micah, sounding content as ever.

"I see we finally *feel* the same. Have fun out there, you two. And please don't dance like twelve-year-olds. Touching *is* allowed at The Experience."

Micah let out a groan and spun Laurel toward the center of the room, saying to Ryan, "You're going to owe me."

"By letting you handle the next time this building takes a shit?" Ryan spread his arms wide. "It's all yours, *amigo*."

"My eyes will fall off if I watch this," April teased and turned in the direction of the bar. "Come find me when you're done, Laur."

"You really must not like dancing," Laurel said once enough distance sat between them and the other two, resisting the urge to smooth her fingers over the tight purse of Micah's lips. "Either that or…it's me you don't want to dance with?"

God that sounded pathetic. Would it really matter if he didn't? But then why would he have invited her?

Her mind seriously needed to stop acting like a love-struck teenager. Sure, she was attracted to Micah. And sure, she was letting him satisfy her in ways she hadn't let a man in…who knows how long?

"The hottest woman in the room? I'd be stupid to not want to dance with her." No physical touch with the admission, but still Laurel let out a tiny breath. The hottest in the room? Did he really think that? "Suffice it to say," Micah continued, "I don't exactly have a *Dancing with the Stars* body type. Can you imagine me swinging and gyrating my hips?"

He had a point. But then again— *I can think of plenty the rest of his body might be good at.* Starting with the appendage just below those hips… "Well," she said, stepping onto the slightly raised dance floor, "if my two left feet can do it, then I'm sure you'll have no problem."

Micah laughed. "The uncoordinated bar owner and clumsy nanny. We might turn into free entertainment for all these people. Ryan would love that."

"Only if it keeps people from leaving." Laurel stopped in the middle of the dance floor and stood, her hands hanging to her sides. Should she reach for him? Start dancing alone? The thought of how awkward this would be hadn't dawned on her until then, but…yeah, it was. "My guess is we'd scare everyone away."

Slowly, carefully, Micah stepped in close and fit his palms over her hips. He smiled and leaned his mouth to her ear. "The place to ourselves?" he said in a low, husky voice. "Now that sounds like a party." His hips started swaying to the beat of the music, his hands guiding Laurel's to match the movement, and too soon she forgot all about the people clustered at the outskirts of the room, at the bar, and now in line for the single coed bathroom.

Even with her heels, she had to tilt her head to look up at him. A few inches of added height, yet she still felt so small next to him. Vulnerable. Exposed. Especially with the direct access he had to her bared neck.

His stubble brushed against her cheek. Soft lips pressed into the skin just below her ear, and the torrent of chills rushing across her skin was enough to start that low burning in her belly. His hands slid up her sides, the tips of his thumbs brushing lightly against the edges of her breasts, and in unison he positioned one leg between hers, his knee firm and tight against her center.

Fire erupted. Her knees weakened. The trail of his hands

continued around her ribcage and down her back, throwing her into a dream-like trance—one where her breath was hard to find and tendrils of sensual pleasure warred with the primal compulsion to rip off his clothes.

The closer she moved to him, the harder his leg pressed into that heated spot, and thank god the music was bumping hard and people were starting to venture out onto the dance floor because it was the only way she could disguise the fact that she was practically dry humping his leg.

Not that he seemed to care.

Growing more insistent, his hands traveled over the waistband of her shorts. Yes, she wanted his hands there. She wanted his hands *everywhere*.

He pulled her in close, every inch of her body pressed against his, and growled into her ear with a teasing chuckle. "This watch of mine. I bet you didn't know it's magic."

She tilted her head away, his warm breath and husky voice threatening to make her insides combust. But she laughed, because she'd never seen him let loose and joke before. "A *magic* watch?"

His eyes met hers, searching. Piercing. "Yep."

"And what does this magic watch say?"

He grinned slyly, running his hands down her back and over the waistline of her shorts. "It says you aren't wearing any panties."

She rolled her eyes playfully. "I think your watch must be broken." Of course she had underwear on.

He shrugged. "Hm, maybe it's an hour fast then." The intensity of his gaze could've dropped her panties right there in the middle of the dance floor. And suddenly words were spilling out of her mouth without her control.

"Or maybe it's only five minutes fast…" The room seemed to stop. And so did Micah's breathing. It was this very moment that she realized she didn't care who was in the room, or who saw her with Micah. This craving she had for him was much too powerful. She stood on her tiptoes and nipped his bottom lip with her teeth, breaking the intense spell her words had put him into.

"Come with me," was all he said and towed her off the dance floor. Heavy bass beats thumped around them then faded to a murmur as they stalked down the hall, past the broken bathroom, and into Micah's small office.

The door slammed.

Her backside hit the wall.

And his mouth was on hers quicker than she could say *holy shit, this is hot.*

His tongue swept in. His hands jerked down the thin straps of her tank then bra, and in only seconds she was completely consumed with him. He was everywhere—palming her breasts, filling her mouth, pinning her to the wall.

This was what she wanted. This was where she wanted to be.

With his massive arms, he gripped below her rear and easily lifted her to his waist, guiding her legs to encircle him. Not that she needed the support—his body was solid as a brick wall—but she wound her arms around his neck to close the space between them. Every inch of her body screamed to be touching him. Soaking him in. Savoring him.

Fire. Was this how it felt to be burning from the inside out?

It wasn't the type of kiss she could get lost in. No, this kiss—exacting and demanding—drew her mind into herself.

Pointing to all the places it was affecting.

The tips of her fingers. *Here.*

At the base of her throat. *And here.*

The very place their two bodies connected. *Definitely here.*

"Micah," she broke away from him and said, gasping for breath at the same time. "Please take off my clothes."

His lips grated up her neck. "No."

"No?" She eased back and met his eyes—so dark and greedy. If she didn't know him, it would have scared her. "But I thought—"

"Oh, we're absolutely doing that. But this isn't the time for school-girl manners." His lips returned to her neck and then his teeth, grazing along the sensitive line he'd just devoured. "If you want your clothes off, you'll have to demand it."

Demand it? Was he serious? "Okay," she said, suddenly unsure. She chewed on her lip for a moment, trying to find the words. They were right there, handed over by him, but she'd never before said anything like that to a man. And it was unnerving. Finally she took a breath and spit them out. "Take off my clothes."

A low chuckle echoed in her ear. "That was hardly convincing, if you ask me."

Her insides were about to explode. Her body about to crumble. She scowled at him. "I *didn't* ask you."

"It's a shame," he said, raising his hands into the air. The weight of her body caught on his waist and braced harder against the wall. "I was really looking forward to..." He shook his head, a teasing grin pushing at his lips. "Guess it doesn't matter anymore."

Ugh, this was maddening! Fine, if he wanted demanding, she'd give him demanding. She took his face in her hands, gripping tight and forcing him to look straight into her eyes. "Micah Crane, take my *fucking* clothes off." It came out more as a growl. *Better than screaming it for all to hear.*

The smile of his that followed—devilish and full of gluttony—sparked something dark inside Laurel. Right or wrong, proper or not, the glint in his eyes smeared those lines until it was all a jumbled mess and there wasn't any distinct box to fall into.

Freeing. That feeling was completely and utterly freeing.

His hands slipped beneath the edge of her shorts and gripped her rear firmly. "As you wish." He swung her around, crossed the room, and propped her at the edge of the desk. Her shirt was over her head before she knew he had even reached for it, her bra shortly following, and then he nudged her shoulders until she was lying back, the glossy wood cool against her skin.

Her shorts were next, her silky thong trailing after that. Only a minute to strip her bare, yet it had felt like an eternity. She looked up at him, at the way his massive body silhouetted in the ceiling lights. To anyone else, he might've looked terrifying—the daunting type a girl certainly wouldn't want to find hovering over her naked body. But to Laurel, Micah's broad shoulders and all-encompassing stature enfolded her like a protective blanket.

"Fuck, Laurel. Why do you have to be so goddamn stunning?"

She giggled and reached for his belt. No man had ever talked to her that way—in fact, no man had ever wanted to screw her in the back of a bar, either—and it sparked a wicked rush through her.

He caressed her thighs, running his hands roughly up the front of them, then wrapped his fingers around her waist and tugged her closer to him. He lifted her legs and draped them over his shoulders, her weight braced on the upper half of her back and her opening tingling at the thought of him being so close to it.

He grinned mischievously, sliding one finger slowly along her folds. The barely there pressure stole her breath, and when he did it again, her mind went with it.

"You have no idea how long I've been thinking about this beautiful pussy of yours. How I've wanted to do this"— he braced his hands on her inner thighs to spread them wider, dipped forward, and licked her clit—"again."

Hot breath stroked along her skin, little white stars swimming in her vision. Suddenly, she was unsure if she could endure another mind-blowing session of his tongue on her in that way. One measly lick and she was already see-ing spots.

"Is it okay, Laurel, if I lick your pussy?"

She whimpered, forcing out a breathless "yes." Her hands flew to the edge of the desk on either side and gripped hard, as if she would fly off the glossy surface the moment his mouth touched her again. "Just please don't make me ask you for it."

He chuckled. "I wouldn't dare." He leaned in closer and kissed the inside of her thigh, tingles zipping and firing in all directions. "But…" Another kiss, this one on the opposite leg. "…you are going to have to *demand* it. Tell me to lick your pussy."

She groaned. "You're maddening."

"And you're going to say the word 'pussy' or spend the rest of the evening enduring the endless torture of wishing you had." His eyes zeroed in on her and glinted. He was teasing, of course, and she knew why. Get her to relax, to step out of her box. She doubted he truly expected her to say it.

Any other time the word "pussy" would have her cringing. But coming from Micah's mouth, in his low, sexy tone, had her spitting out the words before she could think twice about it. "I want you to lick my pussy and suck my clit and make me come hard and fast on your mouth."

Way more than he'd planned, obviously, by the way his eyes grew rounder. A turn on, too, by the devilish smile that followed. His hands flattened along the base of her back. "I won't let you fall. Spread your legs wider."

She could hardly breathe because those words made the sweet spot between her legs swell. She did as he said, propping her ankles on his shoulders and letting her knees fall outward. Bared completely for his taking. And that's exactly what he did.

First a tender trail of kisses then a soft lick, and once his mouth covered her entirely and his tongue darted between her folds, the threat of bursting from the inside out weaseled closer.

His tongue plunged in and out of her, swirled around her sensitive nub then plunged again, and the combination of sensations had her panting in mere seconds. "Tell me how it feels," he demanded against her flesh. Teeth grazed lightly. He sucked her nub hard.

It felt so good, there was no way she could manage speaking at that moment. Her lungs seized and released, her words shaky as she said, "It's like my body is flying and falling all at once." Normally with an orgasm so close, talking would've halted all forward movement, but telling him what her body was doing in the very moment she was about to spill over the edge slammed the wash of pin-prickly pleasure into her tenfold.

She gasped, and then rode the wave until her body went limp.

Slowly he lowered her to the desk. Her eyes closed, the jangle of his belt buckle echoed in the room, then the brush of denim along his skin, and she grinned. Him inside of her, fully and completely…yes, that was what she wanted.

The crinkle of foil came next, and then his hands were on her, dragging her to him. He positioned the head of his massive erection at her opening and looked down with dominant, hooded eyes—eyes that said he would own her the instant he slid inside of her—and grinned.

"Think hard, Laurel. Are you sure this is what you want?"

Hard.

Want.

Sure.

"Positive," she said, propping herself up on her elbows. She wound her fingers around the base of his penis and tugged gently, holding tight against him as—millimeter by millimeter—he entered her. Once buried to the hilt inside her, he held still, giving her a moment to adjust, but more a moment to relish the sweet wave of chills that rose up all over her body. One thrust, and he'd found that sensitive spot.

The one his tongue couldn't reach earlier.

The one that was impossible to find with some men.

As if to put an exclamation mark on that fact, Micah pumped once then paused back where he'd been, hot, sharp tingles jolting out from her core. Her insides contracted at the same time her hands gripped the edges of the desk. Her mind was telling her to do one thing, her body another. But she couldn't hear what either of them was saying because that feeling in between her legs overpowered...*everything*.

Micah planted his hands on the desk, one on each side of her, and ran a trail of kisses along the valley of her breasts before taking them fully into his mouth, one at a time. The pressure inside her short-wired her senses until all she could see, smell, and feel was him.

Drowning... It was like she was drowning in everything that was *him*, yet it was his arms that held to her tight, his hands now on her cheeks, fingers threaded into her hair. He took her mouth with his, traced his tongue over her lips until they parted and he dove in. Below, his body started to move simultaneously, a delicious friction forming with the effort.

Her hips matched his movement as much as they could under the weight of him, tiny gasps of pleasure fluttering off her lips each time he buried himself farther inside her. In his arms, surrounded by him, overwhelmed by him, she felt... she felt...safe. Like he would never let anything in the world happen to her.

Her heart cracked at that thought, and the rest of her body let go completely. As if her cells knew they were safe to open and explode and release. She trembled. Shuddered. Then relaxed into the hard surface of the desk. *Dear Jesus, how am I ever going to recover from this?*

Strong arms scooped her up and carried her to the desk chair. Micah sat, straddling Laurel's legs over him. He took her breast into his mouth and whispered around it, "You are the most beautiful woman I have ever met, Laurel."

A small laugh shook her chest. "Do you say that to all the girls who straddle you in the back office of your bar?"

Both his hands planted firmly on her hips, his fingertips pressing into her skin. *Leave a mark on me, Micah. That way I'll know this is real.* "You're the only person I've ever brought back here," he said. "So I guess that means yes."

His words, and the relaxed look of his face as he said them, filled her. Consumed her. And she wanted him to feel what she just had. The going under. Being entirely overwhelmed by a single person. So that was what she did—fixed her arms around his thick neck, pressed her breasts in his face, and rode the shit out of him until he grabbed hold of her, pumped hard into her, and called out her name.

They sat in the silent room for a moment, catching their breath and waiting for their heart rates to return to something that didn't feel like it was being propelled by something illegal. Micah didn't say a thing, and after a few minutes he stood, lifting her to her feet. He found her clothes and helped her into them, and once she was dressed, he took her face in his hands.

His soft, wet lips fell on her neck, both sides of her jaw, and then her forehead. Finally, he looked down into her eyes for a long moment, then leaned in and pecked her lips delicately.

She blinked, his fingertips feeling as if they were touching her with the sensations of a hundred thousand million hands. But it wasn't his touch that knocked into her like a timbering tree. It was the thought that came just before he let go.

I think I'm falling for you, Micah.

It was way more intense than he'd expected — having Laurel fully. Completely. Up until now, messing around with her had just been like scratching an itch; satisfying, but he'd forget about her the minute she left at the end of summer. But…as he'd helped Laurel into her shorts, then bra, then shirt and watched her straighten everything in preparation to exit back into reality, the more he realized he didn't want her to leave. Didn't want her to move on. The time they'd spent together had been slowly gouging a mark into his heart — enough to know that it might be impossible to forget the beautiful doe eyes that stared at him like he was everything in the world.

The thought scared the shit out of him. Up until now, the only thing that had terrified him was failing Shae. Not being the father she wholeheartedly deserved and giving her the best life possible. But now Laurel was here, and every time he thought of her, saw her, touched her, it was like he was losing a war. One he didn't even know he was fighting. Being with her was like being in a cloud, where everything became distorted and fuzzy with no definite edges.

That cloud carried him into the long hours of the night, and once back home, after he'd thanked and paid Mrs. Briggs for watching Shae, then said good night to Laurel as she was pulling her bedding from the basket beside the couch, he collapsed onto his bed.

The Experience seemed to be a success with a better-than-expected turnout and ecstatic partner. They hadn't calculated their profit yet, but based on the fact that many of their specialty drink ingredients had run dry a good hour before last call hinted to something they'd be smiling over tomorrow.

He lay back on his pillow, the darkness of the room and stillness of the night settling around him. How long had he slept in this room, alone and staring at the ceiling like this? So why did it suddenly feel too dark? Too lonely?

It wasn't a conscious thought to get up and walk to the edge of his room, but as soon as the door opened and his footsteps padded down the hall, he knew exactly where he was headed.

In the living room, Laurel was already sprawled out in the couch bed with the lights out, the blanket crumpled at her feet, and her arms resting above her head. He couldn't tell if her eyes were open or not. Wouldn't have mattered either way.

He approached without slowing, then leaned down and scooped her up into his arms.

"Oh my gosh, what are you doing?" Laurel whisper-shouted with a startled laugh.

Curling his arms upward so her face would be in front of his, he nibbled her lower lip and spun for his room. "Couldn't sleep. Thought maybe you'd have a remedy for that." His steps were silent under the echo of his heart beating in his ears.

For a breath of a moment, she stared up at him. Then she ran her fingers down the side of his face, the slight scrape of her fingernails leaving tingles in their wake. "I might be able to come up with something."

He nudged the door to his room shut with his foot then laid her out on his bed, the loose T-shirt covering her flinging up at the sides, revealing a sliver of milky smooth skin that he suddenly wanted to run his mouth over. He pushed up the material and placed a brief kiss in the center of her stomach, just below her belly button. Then he lowered on top of her and brushed back her hair, looking her in the eyes. "I was thinking," he said, dropping a kiss onto her jaw, "tonight was the first night off you've had since coming here." He kissed her softly before adding, "And it hardly seems fair that it should have to end so soon."

Laurel shook her head, not understanding what he was talking about but loving his breath against her face just the same. His hand slid up her shirt and his palm met her skin, continuing upward until he was cupping her breast.

"You must be really worn out, watching Shae day in and day out like that."

She tried to shake her head, but with her long hair trapped beneath her shoulders it was barely a movement at all. "I'm fine."

That might've been a lie. Watching after a six-year-old 24/7 was more work than she'd anticipated.

His lips left her neck, and he looked her in the eyes. "You're a bad liar," he said, tracing the curve of his knuckles over the thin layer of her sports bra. Right over her nipple. "I know how hard it is to watch her. I know how tiring it can be." He dropped his mouth until it was pressed against hers so gently she hardly even felt it. "I just need to kiss you for a little bit. Then I want you to roll over and get some sleep." His mouth touched hers again, but the way his lips moved couldn't even come close to what his words just did to her.

He wants to take care of me?

Whoever knew that could be such a turn-on?

But *holy hell*, it was so hot.

His hands slipped under the elastic band of her bra, and his mouth covered hers. Each time his tongue slid against hers, it sent her head in a whirling, dizzying spin and stole another bit of her breath. *Will that ever get old? The way he steals my ability to think?*

He may have just said all they were going to do was kiss, but to her, what they were doing was much more than kissing. His mouth was everywhere. So were his hands. He drove the material of her shirt up above her bra, then moved the bra up too, exposing her breast. His tongue teased her, warm and drawing quiet whimpers out of her.

Running his hand down her stomach and over her tight cotton shorts to her thighs, he—at the same time—propped himself up on his elbow, hovering above her, the weight of his leg dipping the bed between her legs. Fingers reached the insides of those legs and then scraped their way to the material between them and her head fell back and eyes slammed closed and—

Oh. My. God. This is the hottest kiss I…

have…

ever…

had.

He began kneading his hand into her, firmly pressing against her shorts until every inch of her body was—not very silently—begging for him. His mouth slid to her neck and kissed and sucked and nibbled, all in the same spot, as if he was trying to claim it. Claim her. Without moving in any way, he slipped his hand under the waistband of her shorts and over the top of her underwear and if she'd known losing one small layer would have increased the intensity this much, she would've requested it minutes ago.

"Fuck, Laurel. You're soaking wet." One finger hooked around the edge of her underwear and pulled them to the side. "I need to feel you."

And then she died.

Or came alive.

She couldn't even tell as his finger slipped inside her and sounds tumbled off her lips and then as he kissed her gently, muffling all her noises as her body crumbled beneath his hand. The fire that shot through her body was so intense and drawn out that she clung to him, afraid for him to move his hand. *Just leave it right there, Micah, and let me sleep with it.*

A minute passed, and then another, and their bodies were absolutely still with the exception of their chests rising and falling heavily. Their eyes were still closed and their lips were still touching, but they weren't kissing. They were just…surviving. Or she was, anyway.

After a few moments, he pulled his hand out of her shorts, kissed her once more on the lips, then rolled her over and tucked her body into his, wrapping his arm around her.

"Wait." She peeked over her shoulder and asked, "What about you?"

He grinned, his eyes glinting even in the darkness of the room. "I don't see any need to keep score." He tugged her closer, the warmth of his body caressing her clear down to her toes. "Now, go to sleep."

Chapter Eleven

Laurel grabbed her keys then knocked lightly on Micah's closed bedroom door—the harsh sound against the wood suddenly throwing her back into the memory of being in his office at the bar, pressed up against the door with his body supporting hers. The memory faded into her lying on his bed this morning, when she'd woken up alone, in his sheets, smelling like she'd submersed herself in everything *him*.

A loud *creak* pulled her back to the hallway. She blinked. The door swung wide, and Micah's massive body filled the entire space. A shirtless, tattooed chest stared at her—one that in all the times they'd been together, she'd never seen completely bare. She'd only gotten glimpses of the tattoo peeking out from the collar of his shirt, though the words "and miles to go before I sleep" scripted around the edges of a solid black compass rose wasn't at all what she'd expected. She was curious what it meant, but at the same time didn't want to know. Did it have something to do with the fighting?

Instead her gaze traced down his torso, across the muscles that rippled along it, down, down, down over the trio of reddened fist-sized blotches on his left side and then even farther to where those muscles formed a V and disappeared beneath his low-slung jeans. The sight alone made it difficult to breathe, but not because of how appetizing he looked.

"You were punched?" Laurel inhaled through her nose, trying to quell the sudden panicky feeling prickling up from her stomach. So that was why he'd left in the early hours of the morning? To fight?

Micah ran his hand through his hair, the lifting of his arm revealing two more—and much darker—blotches marring his skin. "That's nothing you need to be concerned with," he said, his voice firm, but not as harsh as it had been in the past.

She stepped forward and caressed the side of one finger as lightly as she could over the welts. "Do they hurt?"

He stiffened under her touch. "I'll be fine."

Of course he would be fine, they were only welts. But that wasn't what she'd asked. "I know…but do they *hurt*?"

His hand covered hers, stilled her movement. She waited for the moment he would shove her hand away. Waited and waited. Then he gently lowered her hand back to her side. "Can't say they feel good."

The relaxed look on his face filled her with so many emotions it was impossible to categorize them. She was sad at how unaffected he was by the whole fighting situation. Angry about it too. And beneath that sadness and anger, something thicker and fuller and heavier pressed in on her chest. What would happen to Shae if one day Micah didn't return from a fight?

The threat of tears stung her eyes. The precious six-year-old, already missing a mother, without a father too? The thought had her speaking before her mind could catch up. "I'm quitting this job."

"You *what*?"

She sighed, trying to sort out the thoughts her mind was throwing at her. "You said the money from your side job paid my salary, but if this is the result of you trying to pay me with blood money, then I don't want any of it. I quit. I'll finish out the summer with you, because it's what I agreed to do and I don't want to see Shae spending the rest of the summer at the bar, but I don't want your money."

Brown eyes, darker in the dim light of the apartment, assessed her up and down. Her turquoise sandals. Jean skirt. Up to the simple black tee and arrow necklace, then they landed on her eyes. For a minute he just stared at her, his face an expanse of nothingness. No expression at all. Then he pointed at his welts and laughed as though he knew pain and to him this wasn't pain. "*This* also pays Shae's school tuition. Should I pull her out of that, too?"

He'd enrolled her in one of the best schools in the city. "Of course not."

Shrugging, he started to step past her but then stopped just in front of her. "Then I guess there's no need to discuss this further." His eyes grew soft and the intensity in his expression disappeared as his hand reached for her face. She thought he was going to caress her...

Kiss her...

Take her into his arms and surround her with that feeling of safety she'd been consumed with last night...

Rather he swiped his thumb along her cheek and pulled away, showing her a smear of pink lip gloss. *Oh.*

"Shae was putting her Barbie makeup on me," she explained, fiddling with the keys in her grip. Surely the metal ridges were leaving tiny indentations in her palms, considering every single part of her, from her head to her toes, just tensed. "Guess I didn't get it all off. Thanks." She forced her body to turn and, with her heart suddenly crowding her throat, started down the hall.

One step. *Why do I get so flustered when he's near me?* Two. *And why can't I carry on a normal conversation with him without thinking of how much he flusters me?* Then three, four, five. *Without thinking about how much I want him to—*

"Laurel," he said softly.

She almost pretended she didn't hear him just so she could stay in her head a little longer, so he'd have to say her name again. Instead, she spun around and faced him, pretending to be completely unaffected by this man.

"Yes?"

He gestured to the keys in her hand. "Are you going somewhere?"

Right, the reason she'd knocked on his door in the first place. She nodded. "Shae and I are going to get some groceries. We'll be back in a little while."

He answered so fast it was like he hadn't thought about it at all. "I'll go with you," he said.

The wheels on the cart turned, barely clearing the free-standing display of stacked cracker boxes. A millimeter to the left and the boxes would have collapsed. Laurel popped her head down to the cart's lower rack where Shae was crouched. "Sweetie, I don't think I'm strong enough to push your big-girl body around the store like this. Do you mind walking? You can help me put stuff into the cart."

Through the long frizzed-out hair drifting around her face, the little girl gripped the metal supports and smiled innocently. "Good thing we brought Daddy, then. He's strong."

A gentle hand wrapped around Laurel's side, fingertips fluttering light as a butterfly's touch against her waist. She stiffened and tried to ignore the feeling of his hand on her. She tried to focus on the groceries and the aisle and the cart, but Micah's face was so close to hers, and she could feel his breath on her cheek as he said, "I'll push it."

Every tiny hair along the back of her neck rose. Carefully she twisted from his grip, stepped out of the way, then nodded. "That's probably a better idea."

They cleared two aisles, Laurel adding ground turkey and black beans for tacos into the cart then portabellas and marinara for a new stuffed-mushroom dish she was going to introduce to Shae. At the end of the aisle, as Laurel grabbed frozen fruit for the smoothies, Shae smashed her face against the frozen food case.

"Daddy, can we get those chocolate popsicles?"

Micah grinned at his daughter. "Only if you don't eat them all like last time, princess."

Shae giggled. "I promise. Can we get the cookie ice cream too? It's my favorite."

"Pick out anything you want."

Shae grabbed both, Laurel just standing and watching. Was he really allowing her to pick out more than one treat?

Didn't he realize the high number of school-aged children who were obese were that way because of their parents not teaching them healthy eating habits?

"Shae, sweetie," Laurel said, crouching down to her level, "that's a lot of junk food. Why don't you just pick one?"

Shae's bottom lip pushed out. "Daddy said I could get two."

Right…and who was she to go against her father's word?

"Something wrong?" Micah asked, leaning his elbows onto the cart handle. The edges of his sleeves stretched with the movement.

Laurel shook her head. "No."

Micah lifted a single brow. "Have I told you that you're a bad liar?"

Yes, he had, right before he'd made her mind explode with pleasure last night. Before he'd said he just wanted to kiss her for a little bit. Suddenly tingles of heat pierced beneath her skin. "I…um," she stuttered out. She cleared her throat. "I was just thinking that next time Shae asks for junk food, maybe you could take her to the fruit aisle and make it a game. Like ask her to find something sweet and red. That way she thinks she's in charge of picking out the sweets."

"Fruit?" Micah gave her a funny look, as if he had never thought of making his daughter eat fruit. That couldn't have been it, but it was what it looked like. And it made one thing very, *very* clear: she may have quit working for Micah, but there was no way she could leave him and his daughter.

They continued down each aisle, the last containing a variety of school and office supplies. Micah grabbed a few things he thought Shae might need for the start of school: some pencils, crayons, a pink pencil box. Then he told Shae to grab a package of red pens. "For Laurel's classroom," he said to her.

"Actually," Laurel said to him, at the same time taking the package from Shae and returning them to the shelf, "I'm planning to ban red pens from my classroom."

He scratched at his temple. "Aren't red pens mandatory in a classroom? You know, for grading papers, failing people."

"That's exactly why." Laurel sidestepped the cart as Micah turned it toward the check-out lanes. "Did you know people, especially children, feel an unmistakable sense of anxiety at that very moment a teacher hands back an assignment corrected with red ink? I read a study in one of my college courses."

Micah shrugged. "Seems ridiculous the color of a pen would cause that. Maybe it's just the anticipation of knowing how they did."

Shaking her head, Laurel said, "There've been tests done. Blue or green ink versus red. It's definitely the color." She smiled over the cart at him. "So no red pens. Not for grading papers, anyway. It's the least I can do."

The glint in her eyes said it all: Laurel wanted so badly to make a difference in kids' lives—even down to the color of pen she used to check their papers and the way she'd tried to quit her job with him and work for nothing. Being near her and her dreams for the future made Micah both hate himself and want to be a better man.

No changing the world on his part—not unless he counted increasing alcoholism with bar sales and beating people into paying their debts. He was the complete opposite of Laurel. Like light and dark. And it amazed him that the two of them could even have a connection. However, they did, and it was growing stronger every day. Every time he was with her, near her, feeling her, hearing her, thinking of her...the thought of becoming something more with her invaded him. Scared the living hell out of him. Because how could he be anything to her with the threat of Russo breathing down his back?

It was the single thought that hadn't left him the entire night, as Laurel lay with her body tucked against his. He'd listened to her fall asleep. He'd listened to her sigh in the middle of the night. And in the morning he'd kissed her on the head as he'd texted Russo to meet him in the park.

But one mention to Russo about getting out had landed him five punches to his side: one for knowing too much, one for doing too much, one for being a liability, and another for knowing names. The last was for bringing it up in the first place.

Micah knew he needed to get out from under Russo's hand, but...he just didn't know how to do it.

"Well," he said to Laurel, his voice more unforgiving than he'd planned, "I received plenty of tests covered in red and never had any anxiety. Papers too. What would that study say about me?" He didn't know why he was challenging her. Talk of when he was younger, though he'd brought it up, stirred a tornado scratching the inside of his chest. That, and with his admission of being a total fuck up as a kid, was like a double punch to the face.

A girl like her deserved someone much better than he could ever be.

From the roundness in her eyes and crimped forehead,

Laurel was clearly trying to figure out what his deal was. She folded her arms across her center, pink fingernails that Shae must've painted by the mess around the edges glistening in the fluorescent lighting. "I can't tell if you really want me to answer that."

Micah gritted his teeth. No, he didn't. "I'll tell you what the goddamn study would say. That no parental support at home leads to no motivation in the student, which leads to failing grades and shit for an attitude." His hands gripped the cart handle harder. "Changing the color of the pen wouldn't have done a thing for a kid like me."

She blinked up at him, but was smart enough not to argue more of her point. Maybe that idealistic state of mind shit worked on people like her—who'd been raised in a normal family environment. But not him.

Silence pressed in on them as they checked out and even on the drive home. Shae was clearly aware that Micah was pissed by the way she lightly tapped his arm when asking if she could have another Fudgsicle after finishing the first. "Have as many as you want," Micah told her.

Laurel stopped mid-kitchen, a handful of groceries cradled in one arm, head tilted to the side. "Two Popsicles? Don't you think that's a bit much? Especially right before dinner?"

Micah jammed his hand through his hair, unable to control the way every muscle in his body tightened. "Do you really think one more Popsicle is going to make a difference?"

"Yes." Laurel lowered the bags to the counter and faced him. "Just like I think giving her everything she asks for is damaging."

"*Damaging*?"

Laurel nodded. "Micah, I know you're just trying to show

your daughter that she's the star of your world. And I admit, it's endearing to watch at times, but I also know that given how you were raised, the motivation behind that might be for the wrong reasons. And, yes, I think it's damaging. I think you're setting a bad precedent for when she gets older."

"What I think," he whispered through his teeth, biting against the urge to yell the words he couldn't quite straighten out in his head. This was his life, his apartment, his goddamn refrigerator full of Popsicles, and he didn't need someone pointing out the fucked-up decisions he made when it came to his daughter. Maybe Shae shouldn't be eating two Popsicles; Laurel was probably right about that. But what blurted out of his mouth was something less acquiescent. "What I think is that your opinions aren't entirely welcome."

Laurel reared back, as if his words had actually slapped her across the face. Her lips pinched shut tight and then he saw it—the glisten of tears in her eyes.

What the fuck was wrong with him? And why did seeing Laurel hurt slam a hole right through his chest? For the last six years, the only thing that had terrified him was failing his daughter. But this—Laurel on the verge of tears—injected him with something entirely new. Something that cut into him like the deep slice of a knife.

A wrapped Fudgsicle tapped against Micah's arm, and Shae said, "Maybe you should have it, Daddy. It always makes me feel better."

Or maybe he should just leave, free the two of them of all his darkness.

He snatched the Popsicle then his keys and headed for the door. "I'll be at the bar."

Chapter Twelve

They weren't speaking. Hadn't in a few days, other than uttering whatever was necessary to care for Shae. Micah was a dick, and the fact that he couldn't bring himself to apologize for what he'd said to Laurel the other day—that her opinions weren't welcome—only solidified that.

The words were in his head. The "I'm sorry" and "I'm an asshole" and "I don't think I'll never be this way," but every time he opened his mouth to say them, a vise closed around his throat.

Don't ever fucking apologize for who you are. Damn his father's words. And damn the war they raged inside his head. Because he wanted to tell Laurel he was sorry. He wanted to be back in that place where the two of them could be in the same room without the walls closing in on him. To never be like his father…and to take her in his arms.

Instead, he watched from the couch as his nanny whizzed from room to room in skin-tight yoga pants and a colorful tank that made the blue in her eyes pop like a Caribbean ocean. Dishes, laundry, dusting… Since when did mundane household tasks turn him on so much?

The way she gripped the dish brush the same way she'd wrapped her hand around him. The way she stood over a pile of rumpled clothes on the kitchen table, teaching Shae how to properly fold a T-shirt, reminding him of the night he'd stripped her bare and tossed her clothes to the floor with a swell of pride. In that very moment, when they'd fully shared each other's bodies, they'd shared something else. A connection that had since disappeared.

As the day passed and chores around the house turned to reading to Shae and then reading to herself, the pang of want grew in Micah's heart. He'd had her once, and every cell in his body was screaming that it wasn't enough.

"You know…"

Micah blinked and looked up, Laurel standing before him with one hand clutched to her slender hip and the other waving a small wad of twenty-dollar bills. The hard set of her face was more the look of someone carrying out a business transaction. She had a job to do—take care of Shae—even if that meant subjecting herself to more hurt.

"…I thought we decided *this* wasn't an option."

He wanted her but couldn't have her. What else was there to do?

With a nod of his chin, he gestured to the money he'd left on the kitchen table earlier with her name on a post-it. "If I recall, it was you who decided that. I never agreed to not pay you."

She stepped once toward him then stopped, tossing the wad onto his lap. "I'm not taking it."

Casually, he leaned forward and tucked the money into the waistband of her pants, staring directly into her eyes. It almost hurt—this sharp tension between them. "And I'm not letting you give it back to me. We both know you need the money to start up your classroom and probably for your first month's rent when you move out of here." Besides, paying the money he owed her was the only way he'd have it. "So you can either take it willingly, or I can find a way into your account and I can deposit it there myself."

"How could you—"

"Don't forget I know people."

Laurel shook her head, at the same time letting out a sigh. "Ugh!"

Micah closed his eyes and a few seconds later heard the door to their tiny back patio open and shut. *Damn, why is it so hard to not want her?*

Want?

Yeah, at this point it was more like crave. Need. Dangerous emotions for someone who'd always required control over everything to keep his daughter safe.

When he opened his eyes, he saw Laurel and Shae outside, tossing a ball back and forth. His daughter was a pro using the mitt—he'd taught her a few months ago. Laurel, on the other hand, couldn't maneuver the leather contraption for the life of her. Slipping, twisting…shit, a two-year-old could probably catch better than her.

The sight tempered the achy swelling in his chest. Reminded him of the day he'd taught her how to hold the bat. Brought about that hunger to put his hands on her. Be near her. Look into her eyes and put his lips on hers.

This tension between them…he could fix this. He flung

himself off the couch and joined the girls outside, settling into one of the plastic Adirondack chairs. "You're doing it all wrong," he said to her, his tone gentler than it had been all week. It must've caught her off-guard, because her arm stopped mid-throw and she looked at him.

The softness of her eyes hit him full force, and in that split second of silence something changed inside her. An acceptance. A forgiveness. He couldn't tell, but then she admitted quietly, "I know. I've never actually held one of these before."

"Do you want me to show you?"

Under the swoop of hair across her forehead, her eyes widened. Remembering the bat, too? At least he wasn't the only one.

The corners of her mouth turned up faintly, sending warm coils out from his chest. "Sure."

Just as Micah stood, Shae's little redheaded friend from next door popped her head over the fence and asked if she could come over to play.

"Can I?" she asked Laurel, and Laurel pointed at Micah.

"Remember when your dad is here, he's the one you need to ask."

"Please?" Shae jumped, hands clasped under her chin.

Micah smiled. "Go ahead, princess. Have fun." Shae bolted into the apartment and out through the front door, and once she was out of earshot, Micah turned to Laurel, stepping close and gently cradling her face in his hands.

"I'm not going to apologize for paying you the money you have earned. You deserve every cent, if not more, for the amazing work you've done with my daughter. But I will apologize for being an ass to you."

Already, she was shaking her head. "I shouldn't have judged you for the way you've been raising Shae. And I shouldn't have brought up your past. I know none of that could've been easy—"

"Easy or not, it gives me no right to take it out on you. To tell you that your opinions aren't welcome. Because they are." *They always will be.* He smoothed his thumb over her lips, watching as her blue eyes focused on his and her chest rose and fell with a deep breath.

He wasted no time pressing his mouth to hers. Claiming her lips and tongue in a kiss that left him dizzy and staggering. Too much time separated the last night they'd kissed like this, and god, the touch of her felt so damn unbelievable. She matched his kisses, running her fingers through his hair, fingernails digging into the back of his neck. The sting was like jamming an electric rod down his spine, yet when the aftershock subsided and the pinpricks dissolved, all that was left was a warm, bubbly feeling. He was so full with her in his arms. Bursting with thoughts of carrying her to his bed and making love to her—

No.

Fuck.

Not making love.

That word shouldn't even be allowed in his vocabulary with Laurel. Not unless it was banded with hurt and brokenheartedness and pain—because that was what she was sure to feel with him around. But as she pulled her mouth from his, ran her tongue over her lips, and whispered "Jesus, Micah, I want you," that warmth in his chest budded into an aching heaviness.

He wouldn't love her.

But he could still have her. Just not in his bed.

Nipping her lip, he lifted her to his waist then carried her inside, shutting the vertical blinds to the glass slider first then laying her out over the kitchen table. His hands moved up her legs and then her waist where he gripped his fingers around her form. She smelled so damn good. She felt amazing. And all she was doing was lying on a table.

He leaned down and placed his lips over hers, slipping his tongue into her mouth again. His tongue moved against hers slowly, taking the time to taste her, feel the wetness of her. They breathed deeply into each other's mouths, and unable to deny or resist her, he grabbed each side of her face and pressed her forcefully against him, locking his lips around her. She moaned into his mouth, and he kissed her harder, wrapping one arm beneath her and pulling the rest of her body closer.

Running his hand up her stomach, he bunched the colorful material of her tank top above her soft, fleshy mounds, his tongue watering at the thought of having her pebbled nipples in his mouth. His fingers hooked into the silky pads and dragged them down until, one at a time, her tits popped free. His mouth ravaged one, his fingers the other, all the while tiny, whispered gasps seeped into the air.

"My pants," she gasped out, her hands pushing his down her belly. "Take them off."

Micah chuckled against her skin. If that wasn't sexy as hell... "Demanding today, aren't we?"

She looked at him, her eyes swirling with fire, her fingers still covering his. This close, it was like he could see inside her soul. Like her eyes were the gateway and an invisible tether encircled his neck and dragged him closer and closer.

Christ, what was happening to him? And why did his chest feel like it was swelling? Like it was going to expand and expand until it burst?

Because you're falling for her, dumbass.

Laurel propped herself on her elbows, eyes skimming the entirety of his face. Then a line cut between her puckered brows. "Micah?"

Already have.

No. Fuck. Tightness clenched his muscles as he pressed a single finger over her kiss-swollen lips. "No more talking." As fast as he could, he stripped her free of the tight black pants, tossing them to the floor along with the simple black thong she wore beneath.

Bare legs wrapped around his waist and fastened behind him, but even that felt too intimate. Hands on the inside of her knees, he pushed until her legs detached and spread like a butterfly's wings. Quickly he worked his belt then button on his jeans, snatching the condom from his wallet before dropping his pants.

He covered himself then planted his hands in the crook of her waist and towed her closer. The head of his cock gently pressed into her folds, her back bowing off the table in reaction. He circled the pad of his thumb over her clit as he entered her, plunging deep and hard and unforgivingly.

She gasped, her fingers clawing into his sides. "Micah, you feel so good."

He pulled out and slammed into her again.

"Like slippers on my freezing toes." She giggled. In, out, her hips bucking against his. "Like the first sip of wine after a long day." A smile pushed at her mouth, and she sucked her lower lip into her mouth, her teeth grazing the flesh until it popped back out. He thrust again, watching as pure need poured from her gaze. "Like," she added, quieter this time, "like…the air I breathe."

A necessity to live. That was it. His eyes speared hers, and he growled out, "I said no more talking." He picked up his pace, using the grip around her willowy waist as leverage until she writhed and squirmed beneath him. No matter the feelings bashing around inside of him—the pissed-off, punch-himself-in-the-face cloud growing in his chest or the guilt lining its edges because, well, if feelings were getting involved, then this couldn't happen again—he wanted nothing more than for her to find release. He slowed his pace considerably, pausing with his cock buried to the hilt with each thrust. Lying beneath him, her eyes heavy-lidded and blown to the edges, her face was becoming easier and easier to read. The deeper the thrust, the longer the hold, the slower the exit…the tighter she became. He reached between their bodies and flicked her clit with another painfully slow draw. She inhaled. Held her breath, and on the next dive in gasped out his name.

Fuck, she was gorgeous when she was coming. And panting his name. The combination like the adrenaline rush after a good fight.

The quickened pace returned, with it his release *and* the shattering staccato of words his mind was throwing at him— *She's. Too. Good. For. You*—like pebbles on a glass window.

Hurting her was out of the question.

He knew what he had to do.

Once he'd found his breath, he carefully stood and pulled her up with him. The electric beam in her eyes…he knew what it meant; her feelings were growing for him too.

It wasn't an immediate escape, but after he yanked up his pants, he retrieved hers from the floor and placed them in her hands.

Then he turned and walked out.

Ten minutes. It took him ten minutes to shower, change, and not say a single word as he headed out the door. Tears pricked at Laurel's eyes. Was she really that horrible?

Who knew what kind of women Micah Crane had been with in the past. Based on his ruggedly handsome good looks and astounding, give-a-girl-an-orgasm skills, she was sure there had been plenty. Was that why he'd left her standing in the middle of the dining area? Naked? Because she wasn't up to his standards?

Why does it matter, anyway? It's not like you're in love with him.

Her mind could say things like that all day, but the ache in the center of her chest when he walked out of the apartment made one thing clear. There was unquestionably something there.

Laurel tried to busy herself with the remainder of the household chores, since Shae was with her friend, but thoughts of Micah kept creeping in. The way he'd looked at her, like he'd felt something blossoming between them beyond the sex too. But she had to remind herself that their time together was obviously just a way for him to release his pent-up tension. Nothing more, and it took scrubbing the kitchen for that to sink in.

Nothing more. Nothing more. Nothing more.

Laurel was staring at the living room ceiling, darkness tightening the room until it looked like a hollow tunnel, when she heard the *click* of the deadbolt and the door swing open. Every time Micah was gone—but especially at night— she wondered if it would be him walking through the door or some gnarled-toothed, greasy-looking guy wielding a knife. Micah had said she could be in danger, and for some reason her mind seemed to take that idea and turn all Hollywood on her.

Footsteps thumped along the carpet, and then the over-head light flicked on, piercing her eyes with its brightness. Micah looked at her. She looked at him. Was it possible to be scared by the absence of any look at all?

"I have to kiss Shae good night. Stay here. I need to talk to you." He turned and stalked down the hall, a white envelope peeking out from his back pocket.

Like I have anywhere to go...

A minute passed. Then another. She sat up, pulling her knees to her chest, the blanket covering her bare legs. What could he want to talk to her about? She hadn't seen him since he'd left this afternoon, after they...

Well, after *that*.

When Shae had come home from her friend's house, the two of them had made dinner, read a few stories, colored in a coloring book, then went to bed. Laurel had stayed up reading for a while, but she couldn't fathom what he would want to talk to her about, looking so...upset.

His footsteps echoed down the hall, the crinkle of paper

accompanying the sound.

Micah entered the room, then leaned against the wall with his ankles crossed and folded his arms over his chest—his invisible shield, the one he put up to guard himself from letting her see too much of him. But there was one thing that shield couldn't protect—his eyes. And the hurt she could see clouding like a storm in them. "I thought I could trust you, Laurel."

"You can," she said, with no hesitation at all. *Why in the world would he say that?*

"And I thought that when you took this job, you said your record was clean."

Had she said that? She wouldn't ever have lied. "I…" She sat up straighter. "Wait, how could you know about that?" She'd been assured it hadn't been listed on her background check. Probably would never have gotten hired with the district had it been there.

He stomped forward and unfolded the paper. "I know people, remember?" The paper appeared in front of her, and he pointed to the single word. Eight letters. ARRESTED. "You had me thinking this whole time that your record was clean. That you were someone I could trust with Shae. What the *hell* were you arrested for?"

He didn't like strangers in his private life; April had told her that when Laurel had first moved in with her brother. And by the grimace lingering on his mouth and the color slowly draining from his face, she knew that his fear of letting people into his life was driving him into a slow panic. Or explosion. She wasn't sure what type of reaction was building in the man who towered above her. "Micah…it's not what you think."

"Then tell me what it is," he growled out, every single muscle in his body drawing tight, "because right now I'm thinking you're someone I don't even know. Someone who's led me to believe she was someone else entirely."

He was thinking the worst—a felony of some sort. Prison time. "I was seventeen, visiting my grandparents in Ohio. The neighbors next door had a daughter my age, and we used to hang out when I would come for the summers. One day we were fishing at the river and we met a group of guys and one thing led to another and we ended up getting a fish drunk. Police came and, well, that's what we got arrested for."

He scowled. "For under-age drinking?"

"No. For getting the fish drunk. It's illegal to do that in Ohio. Or…it was seven years ago. I don't know if it still is."

"You got arrested for *getting a fish drunk*?" She could see it in the way his eyes darted back and forth between the paper and her—he wasn't sure if he should believe her.

"Yes," she said. "It wasn't even me feeding the fish beer, but because I was there and no one else would admit to it, we all got charged." She took the paper from him and set it beside her, then glanced back up to him. "It's not in my *official* background check because I was a minor when it happened. And I didn't think to tell you because, honestly, I forgot about it. It was a long time ago."

"That's ridiculous."

A smile pushed at her mouth. "That's what my parents said too."

He folded his arms again, looking hard at her with that uncomfortable stare. Stares like that shouldn't be allowed on enormous and intimidating guys like him. "Anything else in your background I should know about?"

Laurel thought about it. "I once taste tested so many flavors of ice cream that I left the store full and without buying any." She reached up and hooked her fingers in the front pocket of his jeans. He stiffened, and she didn't like that, so she gave him another. "And in college your sister and I got caught after we stole a fire extinguisher and sprayed it in the apartment of a guy who cheated on her. That one was all her. I was just along as best friend support."

His hands settled on her forearms, then ran a slow line to her shoulders. His touch, and being near him…was she going to be able to let this go when it was time for her to leave in August?

Up until now, she'd thought leaving Micah and Shae would be easy. But it seemed the more time she spent with them, the more the strings of her attached to the strings of them. Sorting out and untangling that mess of strings was going to be tricky.

Fingertips walked up her neck and then wrapped around the back of her head. Micah gently tipped her head until she was looking him in the eye. Ever so slightly, he nodded, as if he was answering someone or something in his mind. Then he said to her in a low, firm whisper, "Please don't scare me like that again."

Chapter Thirteen

Keys hit the counter with a *clank*, and Laurel looked up, her eyes growing wider with the sight of Micah. *Shit, maybe I should've cleaned up a bit.* Her eyes scanned his face, lingering on the very place that asshole had gouged his disgusting fingernails into Micah's cheek, then drifted downward to his hands. To the split in his knuckles. The caked-on blood.

She dropped the slice of bread she was holding onto the plate and faced him. "Are you okay?"

A vicious cycle this was—taking more and more jobs to stay out of the house and away from the greedy temptations she presented, but craving the sight of her, the sound of her voice, the feel of her hands on him once it was all over. Everything about her made him feel like a different person, like if they had met in another life, where their time together wasn't limited and blanketed with the threat of Russo's men, that perhaps they could be something more.

"I'm fine," he said then grabbed a beer from the fridge, popped it open, and downed it. Within seconds she was standing before him, a wet paper towel in her grip. She reached up to him, the blond hair falling across her forehead not disguising the worry line beneath. His arms ached to pull her close, feel her warm, slender body against his and the sense of calm her touch brought. Why did she insist on taking care of him? He'd let her last night—she'd wiped the blood from his split lip. He'd also kissed her instead of thanking her with words the way he should have, but all of that only happened because the fight in the alley had completely exhausted him and he'd been too weak to fight that urge to be close to Laurel.

Tonight, he wasn't so tired. Gently, he scooped up her wrist and pushed it away. "Don't."

"Why?"

"Because…" *Because I didn't come home to be mothered. Because it looks a lot worse than it is. Because when you touch me, I fucking melt, and the last thing I need is to fuck up the perfect situation you have with my daughter with the shit fest of my life.* "Because I'm *fine*." He turned for another beer.

"Micah," she said quietly, leaving the wet cloth on the counter, "this is the second night in a row that you've come home bleeding…"

The implication was there: bleeding didn't equate to fine. Little did she know, it did. And being fine meant keeping his head down and getting Russo's douchebags to pay their debts in order to keep the two of them—Laurel and Shae—safe and out from under Russo's eye. Douchebags like the scrawny one from tonight, who'd threatened to teach him a lesson.

"It's my job, Laurel," he said to her. "Please stop acting like you care."

"No, your *job* is at The Alibi. And you need to accept the fact that I do care." The last three words were merely a whisper drifting in the space between them. He could tell by the roundness of her glistening eyes that she meant every one. And that was the biggest problem. No matter what kind of asshole he was to her, she wouldn't stop trying to get back to that place they'd been before.

Saving the world one child at a time. Yeah, well, he was far past saving.

Hands hanging at his sides, he looked her dead in the eyes and hardened his stare. "Then stop that too."

She narrowed her eyes, matching his icy glare. "Why? So your daughter can watch you spiral out of control before her eyes? She's not a baby anymore, Micah. She's six years old. She notices things. The cuts. The bruises. The way you leave at the drop of a text. Is that what you want?"

"What I *want*?" He ran his hand through his hair, sucking in a lungful of air to avoid shouting. "You think I *wanted* to be raised by a man who chose booze and brawling over his own blood? That I *want* to be fighting every night? Sometimes, what you *want* and what you *get* are on different realms of existence." His arms flew out to the sides. "This? It's out of my fucking control."

"But it's not." She stepped toward him, her voice low. "It doesn't have to be—"

"Yes! It does!" Nails, it felt like nails were suddenly piercing his chest. He closed his eyes and drew in a ragged breath. "I can't stop hating my father. But I can't stop being like him, either." Fuck! "There, I said it. Doesn't change a goddamn thing." Was this what she'd wanted? To point out what a fucked-up person he was? He stepped back and snatched up his keys.

Arms crossed over her belly, she scowled at him. "Leaving isn't going to fix this."

A loud, sharp burst of a laugh spewed out of him. "Evidently you missed the whole point of this conversation. I. Can't. Be. *Fixed*."

"Whoa. Did I miss that it was Dress Up Like Shit Day?" Ryan laughed, the bar door slamming behind Micah. "What the hell happened to you?"

Micah seized a clean glass from the freshly wiped bar counter and poured himself a whiskey. "I don't want to talk about it."

"She's gettin' to you that bad, huh?"

Micah's head snapped up, and he pointed to the side of his face that had been scratched. "Laurel didn't do this." Jesus, what kind of nanny did he think she was?

Ryan's eyes brightened. Surely he was smiling, though it was impossible to see beneath the face muff he was sporting. "No shit, Sherlock." He nodded his chin toward Micah's eyes, spearing them with his own. "I was talking about those. You know, for as long as you've been working this side job, you've yet to come in here all 'woe is me, my life sucks.' Shit, usually you're all fired up after a brawl." He dipped another glass in sudsy water, swirled it, dunked it in the clean water then withdrew it and worked a towel around the edges. "For as long as I've known you, I've never seen you so torn up over a girl before—"

"I'm not—"

"Save me the bullshit, brother," Ryan said with a corresponding tone. "She's a nice girl; I don't know what the problem is."

"She's a nice girl. That *is* the problem." He plopped down onto a barstool, a loud *crack* resonating in response. Quickly he stood, noticing a solid spilt through one leg. He shook his head. "Really?"

"That's the second one to break this week. I'm thinking with the profit we made from The Experience, if we hold an event like that a few times a month, we might be able to afford to fix up the place properly, with decent furniture and working toilets." Ryan didn't mention the increase in money being what could help Micah get out from under Russo's hand, which he appreciated. They both knew that money wasn't what kept Micah enforcing. The tethers that bound him to the group snaked so much deeper.

Ryan pointed at Micah. "Let me guess… She deserves better than you. Are you seriously pulling that right now?"

Arms wide out to his sides, Micah chuckled, sharp and with no humor. "Look at my life. Raising the kid who was literally dumped on my porch by a woman who wanted nothing to do with my Boston Alibi life, working in a bar that is practically crumbling in our hands, and under the thumb of one of the biggest crime families on this side of the country. A fucking hooker could do better."

Ryan lifted a brow.

Micah slugged half his whiskey. "No, I'm not comparing her to a hooker. But that's my point. She's so much more, with a really bright future ahead of her. She doesn't need me dragging her down into my world."

"Ever think it was the opposite? Laurel bringing you into her world." He shrugged. "Honestly, it could be good for you. Obviously it has been for Shae."

He couldn't deny that. His daughter was becoming quite the young lady, no doubt because of Laurel. Politeness, etiquette, accountability... Countless qualities that simply didn't exist in Micah's vocabulary. He was like a caveman compared to her. Booze and brawling fueling his every move.

Jesus, what would Shae have ended up like without Laurel's influence? He cringed. Surely, if he'd had a son, the boy would be following in his footsteps. But he could never let his baby girl become what he was. Or become the woman who fell for what he was.

Lips to the rim of the glass, he gulped the liquid. Swallowed hard. "Laurel's world, Ryan? Do we look like we're in fucking suburbia?" A girl like Laurel Harris would *never* end up with a guy like him. He would make sure of it.

"You know what I mean." Ryan dipped another glass, soapy suds clinging to the dark hairs on his arm. "She's all rainbows and unicorns compared to your black cloud."

Micah finished off his whiskey, poured another, then slid the bottle toward Ryan. "Didn't know you were a poet."

His friend stopped the bottle with his forearm and shot him a grinning scowl. "Didn't know you were an ass. Oh, wait. Yeah, I did."

Micah smiled back. "Grade school again."

Ryan uncapped the bottle of whiskey and took a long pull. "Shit, if we were in grade school, you would've had a black eye from fucking with the kids two grades ahead of us." He pointed to Micah's scratched-up cheek. "At least now you have the wits to pick on someone your own size."

No, the guy who'd done that to his face had been much smaller than him. Weight-wise, anyway. But he wouldn't go into detail about it with Ryan. Wouldn't bring him into that world, either.

"Gotta admit, though," Ryan added, the upper half of his face smoothing into a serious expression. "Something's different about you since you hired her. And since you're not admitting to any *feelings*, I can at least say that. You've been different."

Feelings… Damn, the alcohol was stealing his ability to give a shit what he said. "You want feelings, I'll tell you what I feel." Elbows on the bar counter, he clasped his fingers in front of him and sighed. "I don't know what to feel when I'm around her."

"God forbid you were ever on the debate team," Ryan said with a laugh.

"I'm serious." Micah shook his head. "It's like a tornado of confusion when she's around. Every part of me wants her. But there's a snag in my brain that keeps pulling me back, telling me there's no way it could work with her going back to Cambridge for her teaching job in a few weeks."

"You couldn't go with her?"

Micah rolled his eyes. "We both know me leaving this place isn't an option, either."

"Why not?" Two simple words, and they jolted him like a punch to the face.

Micah's eyes snapped up. Because he was too much like his father. Because this was the life he'd chosen, and there was no going back. "The Alibi? You?" *Russo…*

"Don't let this shithole hold you back, man."

In his mind, he tried to picture it. Raising Shae in a track-home neighborhood. Working a nine-to-five job. Living in Laurel's sunshiny world. But that was where his mind jammed. Laurel and Shae fit perfectly. Not him, though. Inserting him into that vision was like taking a can of black spray paint to a brightly colored mural.

Not. Going. To. Work.

"I took on this place with you. I would never dump it on you."

Ryan nodded at Micah's words, or more likely his tone. That was the benefit of talking with the guy who'd known him since they were kids. He knew when to stop.

"Whatever, man." Ryan dried the last glass and stacked it with the others. "Speaking of dumping this place on someone. You think you could close up for me? I've got to get to my mom's. Apparently her cat has an ass hernia."

Micah laughed. "And she wants you to do *what* with it?"

Shaking his head, Ryan held up his hands. "No idea. She's too cheap to take him to the vet."

"I've read you can just push those back in."

Ryan's eyes widened, mouth dropped open. "Fuck that." From his pocket, he tugged out his phone. "I better call her before I show up. My luck is she's been reading whatever fucked-up material you have."

"Good luck with that."

Ryan raced out of the room and Micah laughed. He loved messing with his friend.

Micah slid the key from the lock and shoved it into his pocket, the cool, middle-of-the-night air trickling down his neck. Another so-so night in the bar. A handful of customers each hour, but nothing to tip the gains scale—

The sudden feeling that someone was standing behind him coursed through his blood, cold and disconcerting. Quickly, he packed the ring of keys in his hand, maneuvering one between his middle two fingers, and spun.

A familiar face stared back at him—black and blue thanks to Micah's fist earlier that day. Micah cocked his head and smirked. "You come back for more, asshole?" Blood still caked the guy's white shirt, running a broken line clear down to where it stretched over his mini-spare tire. A quick glance to his empty hands ensured the bastard hadn't come back to flaunt something deadlier. No gun. No knife. So why was there a bilious fizz bubbling in his stomach?

"Told'ya I'd be teachin' yous a lesson."

"With that grammar, I don't think you should be teaching anybody anything. You here to give back my cheek skin, pussy?" Micah threw his shoulders behind him and didn't wait for his answer, using the brunt of his forearm to clear the path of douchebag. "I know six-year-olds who can fight tougher than you."

Yellow light puddled sporadically throughout the vacant parking lot, moths ticking against the glowing bulbs. The eerie silence as he stepped away from this guy—what was his name again? Big Joe? Little John?—turned his blood to ice.

Half the guy's mouth turned up in a mangled smile and he swooped his arms, Vanna White style, in front of him. "Can they fight better than these guys?"

These guys?

Out from the shadows, a gang of bodies—*very large bodies*—stalked toward him. At least ten of them. No weapons, Micah noticed immediately, unless he were to count the number of melon-sized fists.

Teach him a lesson. Fuck. His stomach sagged to his knees, and he looked to the swollen, bruised-up face. "A pansy who needs other people to do his dirty work? Guess I should've figured that when you drew claws instead of fists."

Teeth glinted in the light. "Sound familiar?" The bodies strode closer, forming a half circle around him.

"Not an insult to me, dumbass." He clenched his fists, the serrated metal digging into his palm. "I *am* the guy who does the dirty work."

The guy shrugged. "Maybe next time yous should re-search the *pansies* ya decide to beat da shit outta then. Make sure he don't have a band-a-brothers who be comin' to find ya." A true street fighter, this guy was. One who wasn't look-ing for a fair fight, but looking for a win. Shit bags like this would do anything to impose their will, even if that meant calling in every friend he had to pay retribution in the dead of the night. *Fuck, please don't let him have more.* The guys stepped farther into the light, the yellow glow washing their hard-set faces and thin-set mouths to an unnatural, sickly hue. The biggest of the guys shrugged out of his black leath-er jacket, tossed it to the ground, then smoothed his hand over his tattooed scalp—

The hockey game. Shit, these thugs looked just like the group Laurel had pointed out, saying something about the risk of jumping into something with people he knew noth-ing about. They weren't the same guys, of course, but damn if they didn't remind him of that very moment. Remind him that he should've been smart about this assignment, not jumped so desperately into it just to distance himself from the woman he was falling for…

Rule Number Two, according to his father: *Never take on the scrawniest guy in the group. They always have bigger friends.*

Micah knew how fights like this went down. There was no talking his way out of it. No escaping, either, with as many of them as there were. So he did the only thing he knew—widened his stance, rolled his fingers into his palms, and said, "Well…what are you waiting for?"

A crescent of dingy-toothed grins was the last thing he registered before footsteps rushed toward him, drumming as fast as a handful of change clinking to the ground. The bald guy charged first, both arms extended, and slammed his massive body into Micah's chest, pinning him to the bricked entrance of the bar. What was this guy—two-eighty minimum? Jagged rock gouged into the crown of his head. Sour, alcohol-stenched breath clouded in front of his face. He'd fought large-and-in-charge guys like this before. Getting out from against the wall and the upper hand was what he needed to do—

A fist slammed into his jaw from the left. Then another from the right, sending a sharp zinging pulse down his neck and up into his eyes. So this was how they were going to play? His eyes found the skinny one, standing off in the distance, out of arm's reach. "Are your friends really that scared of me? Won't even let me fight fair?"

The face just inches from him growled. "No street-fighting handbook in my pocket, brother," he spewed out. "We're here to make sure you don't mess with our guy again."

The pressure on Micah's chest released, and he instinctively stepped forward, away from the wall. While he didn't care for the possibility of someone coming up from behind, he'd learned long ago empty space was far more of an advantage than somewhere to be trapped.

Teeth gritted together, he scanned the group. Each one staggered from the next, fists tightened. Ready. Just as he inhaled a shallow breath and primed to charge, a few sets of eyes flickered to his left. Micah turned in time to see a branch, bigger and thicker than his arm, swinging. It cracked against his head, and he hit the ground face first, taking in a mouthful of cement. Shoes surrounded him, too many to count. Voices echoed through the ringing in his ears. *Motherfucker. Pussy. Cocksucker.* It was raining spit, and he tried with all his might to make his mouth reciprocate the gesture, but his gasping lungs weren't having it. This wasn't going to be good.

Something smashed into his side. His breath vanished. He choked on his spit. Something else hit his back. Leg. Stomach. Hot blood trickled down his temple, and he tried to look at the guys' faces, but all he could see was shoe after shoe after shoe connecting with his body, leaving smudges of brown along his clothes.

Pulling his legs to his chest, he ducked his throbbing head and covered it with his arms. Less surface area to kick. He closed his eyes. Seconds, minutes, eons. He didn't know how long he grit his teeth against the pain before thoughts of Shae and Laurel inundated his brain. *I failed them. Both.*

Before the cloud of black rescued him.

Chapter Fourteen

"Laurel." The deep voice tugged on Laurel's mind. Jerked her farther and farther from the roomful of noisy kids.

Wait. Roomful of kids?

"Laurel, are you sleeping?" the voice said, louder this time. "Or can you not hear me?" Laurel opened her eyes at the same time the voice in her ear spouted, "Dammit!"

The world slowly faded into view. The ceiling she stared at every night. The glow of her cell phone blushing against the purple couch cushions. The voice in the receiver. "Who is this?"

"Thank God. Damn you're hard to have a conversation with. This is Ryan. From the bar. Micah's friend. Listen, the hospital just called—"

"Hospital?" Her body winched up, sending her head into a dizzying circle. She pinched the bridge of her nose to right the room, then quietly scrambled to the wall in search of the light switch. "Is he okay? Was he in an accident?"

"Not an accident."

"A fight." Her thumb brushed the switch, and she flicked it on. Brightness glared. Along with the sudden drubbing of her heart against her chest and throbbing in her forehead, this had to be the rudest wakeup call she'd ever had. Worse than a bucket of ice water.

"Yeah, a fight. But listen…it's not what you think."

She swallowed. "Ryan, I know about the side jobs. Which hospital?" *How bad could the fight have been?* Her mind suddenly started somersaulting. Broken bones? Split cheek? Unconsciousness? Pressure lassoed around her chest, squeezing, pulling, pushing tight.

Oh god, what if it was even worse than that? A coma? Brain damage?

"Boston Med. Center," Ryan answered. "Emergency room."

"I'll be there as soon as I can." She hung up the phone and sprinted into the bedroom, crouching beside Shae's bed, but then froze. She couldn't let Shae see her father that way—not without knowing how bad it was first.

Mrs. Briggs. She could ask Old Mrs. Briggs to watch her. As fast as she could, she threw on some jeans and a sweatshirt then ran across the apartment breezeway and knocked on the door. *Please, oh please, don't let her sleep heavily.*

She knocked again, this time with the edge of her fist, and an eternity passed before the door creaked open and a tuft of red hair appeared. Laurel wasted no time. "Mrs. Briggs, I don't know if you remember me. I'm Shae's nanny from across the way." The words rushed out too fast. She inhaled a breath. "There's been an emergency with her father, and I need to go see him. Can you sit with Shae until I get back? I promise it won't be long." That last part wasn't exactly true—she had no idea how long she'd be gone, but at least she knew Shae would be safe with the old woman. Micah had trusted her, which meant she could too.

The woman rubbed her face and said in a sleep-worn voice, "Of course, let me just grab my housecoat."

Boston Medical Center was a behemoth of a building, squares upon squares stacked and staggered like Lego blocks. Laurel followed the signs to the emergency room, parked, then burst through the doorway in a much too dramatic fashion.

Okay, slow down. Don't panic.

But her heart was in her throat and her mind was spinning, her breath not filling her lungs fast enough. All she wanted to do was see Micah.

She rushed past the rows of chairs to the counter that read CHECK-IN. Tapping her fingers viciously along the blue Formica top, she watched as the lone nurse slowly glanced up from the stack of papers in front of her, folded her plump arms over the mound, and looked Laurel up and down. "Can I help you?"

Yes, be more on edge. This is an emergency room, is it not?

"I'm here to see Micah Crane. He was in a—" Shoot, not a fight. That wouldn't sound good. She pinched her lips, gripping the countertop. "I mean, he was hurt. I was told he was here?"

Another scan of her weary-looking eyes. *Jeez, did she do this to everyone?*

"And you are?"

His family. She wouldn't be able to see him if she wasn't.

"His fiancée," she said quickly, trying her hardest not to scream at the woman for her to hurry up and let her in. "Please, ma'am, you have to let me see him."

Without a word she shuffled through the papers on her desk. "Micah what?"

"Crane." Laurel sucked in a deep breath through her nose. In the waiting area behind her, someone coughed. A baby let out a wail. Then the door to her right swung wide and a doctor stepped out, calling for the family of a Sarah Randolph.

The nurse cleared her throat. "Micah Crane has been admitted."

"Admitted?" Laurel's lungs seized. *No, no, no.* "How bad is it?"

The woman's fleshy hand, rings circling every finger, motioned to the chairs on the opposite side of the room. "Have a seat over there, and I'll let you know when you can see him."

She was going to have to wait? But... "I'm his fiancée."

"I understand that, miss, but we have to ensure—"

The sound of a deep voice hollering a string of obscenities stole the nurse's words. They both looked in the direction of the voice, where a row of curtained rooms stretched along the far wall. *Oh, no. It's him.* Why was he making a scene? Laurel pointed and smiled politely. "I believe that's my husband-to-be."

Just barely, the woman's eyes widened. Trouble, surely

she wouldn't want any trouble in here. A curt nod, and she whispered, "Come with me." She led Laurel down the linoleum hall, past a number of parted curtains, peeking through each one to look for any sign of Micah.

Finally they came to a halt, the nurse checking the number on the curtain against the clipboard she held against her curvaceous hip. "In there." She leaned close to Laurel. "And please try to calm him."

With a sense of relief filling her, Laurel nodded and quickly slipped through the gap in the curtains. She expected to see Micah lying prone on the bed, with an IV and oxygen tube, of course. The typical first sight of someone admitted to the hospital.

Leave it to Micah to throw that banality right out of the window.

Sitting on the bed with a hospital gown bunched around his waist, too tight against his gigantic biceps, Micah grimaced as he tugged at the IV needle taped to the back of his hand. "Are you finally going to let me the fuck out of here?" he spouted, eyes on the whitish tape holding the needle in place. Hastily, he glanced up, his eyes hard and exacting. "What're you doing here?"

Not exactly the greeting she had been hoping for. "Ryan called me."

His hand stilled and eyes skirted behind her. "Where's Shae?"

Despite the stony glower Micah was shooting her and the little voice in her head warning *uh, oh, he looks mad*, Laurel stepped farther into the room. "I, um, left her—"

His eyes exploded wide. "You *left* her?" He ripped the tape off his hand then started on the needle. It slid out without a sound. "Why did you leave her? What if something happens to her?" The heart-monitor pads popped off his chest next, and he threw them to the end of the bed. Frantic—the man looked frantic.

Hands up, palms facing him, she resisted the urge to throw herself on top of him to get him to stop. "She's not alone. I left her with—"

"One job. You were hired to do one job and one job only," he spat out. Oxygen tube over his head, he stood and swiped off the hospital gown. Every muscle clenching along his brawny torso, he stalked toward her, his face set unyieldingly. "Take care of my daughter. And you left her."

Laurel shrank into herself. *Jeez, he's scary when he's mad.* "I know, but I left her with—"

"I don't give a shit who it was with!" His jaw ticked. He moved closer, hovering his massive body over hers. "And I don't give a shit what you told them. All I know," he lowered his voice and growled, "is that if anything—and I mean any goddamn thing—happens to her, it will be *your* fault."

This was it, Micah's opportunity for an out. A way to send Laurel back to where she fit—miles upon miles away from him. Deep down he knew Laurel was a great nanny and, once the horrendous images of something happening to Shae dissolved, his thoughts zeroed into a single one that started to grow and swell until it pushed everything else out of his brain. *Laurel would be a million times better off without me.* Which meant he had to end their time together. Right now.

He looked down at her now quivering body, lobbing the crushing itch to pull her close and soothe her. To run his hand down her flushed cheek and tell her he was sorry. Standing tall, he stared at the top of her head and said everything he didn't mean. "I refuse to fail again, and anything short of keeping my daughter by my side at all times is a failure." He met her eyes, glistening with tears, and yet he continued, his chest breaking farther and farther apart with each word. "*You* are a failure. Pack your things and go back to the suburbs where girls like you belong."

Chapter Fifteen

Above the trees, the sky was transforming. Traces of daylight bleeding into the pitch black of night, turning the middle of the sky a deep blue. Was it really getting close to morning already?

Laurel rested the top of her forehead against the cool window glass, rocking back and forth as the cab snaked through town toward Micah's apartment. She didn't want to wake April, but she needed to talk.

Through the wetness in her eyes, she found her phone in her purse and dialed.

"Only someone with a death wish would call me this early," April mumbled groggily. "You should know that."

"Your brother's an asshole," Laurel said quietly, emotionally exhausted, but also to maintain what privacy she could in the back of a cab.

"Well, of course he is. He's a Crane. Runs in our blood. And did I just hear Laurel Harris swear?" She chuckled.

She had. And it felt good. She rolled her eyes. "I'm serious. He's the meanest man I've ever met. I shouldn't ever have come here, shouldn't have agreed to work for him." In her heart she knew that wasn't true. Over the last few weeks, she'd grown to care deeply for Shae. Meanest man or not, she was definitely going to miss that funny little girl. The talons clawing into her chest tightened.

"Because you fell for him?"

"Because I...what?" Her eyes snapped wide. "No. I didn't—"

"Spare me the BS, Laur. If there was one thing I noticed last week at my brother's bar event, it was the way you looked at him. And the way he looked at you. There is unquestionably something going on between you two."

Unquestionably...if that wasn't an understatement. The problem was, no matter how much the both of them felt—growing closer as both a couple and a family—they'd both known a time stamp had already decided when things between them would end.

"I may have started to feel something for him," Laurel admitted as the cab pulled in front of Micah's apartment complex. "But that was before he yelled at me and told me I was a failure and that he wanted me to go back to where I came from." Tears pricked her eyes and she wiped at them before digging in her purse for money to pay the driver.

A pause filled the line, and Laurel suddenly hoped April wouldn't ask why her brother had said all those things. She may have been upset at Micah, but that didn't mean she would break her promise to not tell April about Micah's side jobs.

"Wow, that's harsh," April said as Laurel paid the cab

driver and climbed out. "Listen, I know my brother's a bastard—it's sort of just who he is. And I'm sorry you had to see that side of him, but one thing you should know is he only reacts that way when he really cares about something. Or some*one*, if you get my drift. He'll come around. You just need to give him time."

The one—and only—person he cared about was Shae; that much was clear.

Laurel shook her head. "I can't give him any more time." Besides, how could she face Micah after what he'd said to her? "I want to come home."

"Not that I want to be the one to slam more bad news in your face, but your room was rented out last week. A really cute, but sort of nerdy-looking guy. Maybe a little older than us. I haven't had a chance to talk to him yet, but I'm pretty sure he's single because I haven't seen—"

"April?" Laurel interrupted, stepping up to the door. "Can I stay in your room until I figure out where to go?"

"Of course. Call me when you're on your way."

Laurel sighed. At least there was one Crane she could count on.

Inside the apartment, Mrs. Briggs stirred from the corner chair. "How is everything, dear?" she asked quietly.

Laurel stopped mid–living room, scrambling for some semblance of the truth—lying to someone older than her had to be bad karma, right? She ran her hand over her hair, April's errant comment about giving Micah time squeezing her lungs. Could she really leave them—Micah and Shae? Over the last few weeks, she'd seen how badly they'd needed her—

No, not *her*. Maybe someone, but Micah had made it

perfectly clear what he'd really thought of her.

Failure.

Failure.

Failure.

The word haunted her. Was she?

She blinked back to the white-haired woman. "Do you think you could stay until morning? Shae's father likely won't be released until then—" *If he doesn't get arrested for destroying hospital property first...* "And I have somewhere I need to be."

"Of course, sweetie."

"Thank you." Laurel snatched up one of her blankets from the basket beside the purple couch for the old woman then hurriedly gathered up her belongings and stuffed them into her suitcase, her chest growing heavier and heavier with each item she packed. So heavy, it felt as if the floor might cave in beneath her. Heavy, drowning, yeah the list could go on.

Tiptoe quiet, she then snuck into Shae's bedroom and kneeled next to the bed. Telling her she was leaving for good would only upset the little girl, and the last thing she wanted to do was saddle Mrs. Briggs with a hysterical child in the middle of the night. So instead, she kissed Shae on the cheek, whispered that she loved her, and then snuck out.

The deadbolt on the front door clicked, thunderous in comparison to the silence of the early morning. The door creaked and Micah entered, spotting a blanket-covered Mrs. Briggs asleep in the corner armchair.

His neighbor… He shook his head. He should've known Laurel wouldn't have left Shae with just anyone.

Not trying to be quiet, he dropped his keys onto the table, switched on the light, and crossed the room, his black boots thumping with each step. He knelt beside the woman, knowing full well the fucked-up face she was about to wake up to. Those dirt bags hadn't gotten too many face shots in—a few to the jaw and a boot to his left cheek—but on top of the red stripes gouged into the side of his face, he pretty much looked like something out of a horror movie.

Micah was lucky that patrolling cop had seen the one-sided fight when he had. Even though every single asshole had gotten away, at least Micah's unconscious body had made it to the hospital before any permanent damage was done.

Softly, he tapped the old woman's weathered-looking arm. "Mrs. Briggs," he said quietly. Then once again a bit louder. "It's Micah. I'm home now." She blinked open her eyes, taking a moment to focus on his face.

"You don't look so good, dear." She sat up and straightened her fluffy hair. "Is everything all right?"

"Everything's fine." If that wasn't the biggest lie he'd told all day… He swallowed. "Thank you for watching Shae. I really appreciate it."

The woman stood and folded the blanket, her eyes examining his. "That sweet nanny of yours left a little while ago. She was carrying a suitcase."

Micah nodded, quickly shoving that image from his mind. The look on Laurel's face when he'd said those hateful words, pushed her away, was already enough to crumble him. He ushered the woman to the door, thanking her once more.

The orangey glow of morning sunlight trickled into Shae's room, splashing streaks along the floor and up the dresser where the framed photo of the three of them—him, Laurel, and Shae—posing with a giraffe sat. No, he hadn't come in here to wallow. Just to check on his daughter.

He stepped into the room and, at the same time, Shae stirred. "Daddy?"

"Shhh, princess. Go back to sleep." He closed the distance between them and ran his hand over her head. Her eyes fluttered and then locked on his face. Widened.

Shit, my face.

A scream ripped from her mouth, loud and trilling. "Why does your face look like that?" Shae scrambled to the far edge of the bed against the wall, shoving her big teddy bear between them. Legs curled to her chest, she screamed again. "Laurel!"

"No, Shae. Shhh. It's okay. I'm okay. Just a few scratches."

Shae glanced around the room and hugged her knees closer. "Laurel!"

"Baby," Micah said in his most calming tone and sat at the edge of the bed to get closer. He took her hand in his. "Stop screaming."

"But I'm scared." Her round eyes skipped around his face, her forehead crinkling with the threat of tears. "I want Laurel."

How could he say this? That he wanted Laurel too. And that's why he'd let her go. Because his world was too dangerous and she had much greater things to do with her life. He cringed with the words, "Laurel's not here."

"Did you kill her?" Her words rushed out so fast and

unexpected, it took him a moment to register them.

"What? No." How could his own daughter think he was capable of killing someone, let alone someone he cared so much about? Sure he looked like a character from a horror movie, but— *Goddamnit.* "This is just…" He sighed. "I got into a fight at work. But I'm okay. See?" He forced a smile. He was definitely not okay.

"Where's Laurel?"

No way to ease into this one. And he refused to lie to her, either—not after all the shit he'd been through tonight; he just wanted some honesty. And some dignity. He looked his daughter in the eyes and said, "Baby, I sent her home."

"Home?" Shae cocked her head to the side, her voice trembling. "But *this* is her home."

He shook his head, his heart breaking with the sight of his daughter trying to straighten all this out in her mind. She was never going to see Laurel again. His next words drilled in that fact. "This was her temporary home, just while she was working for us and watching you. She went back to her real home. With Aunt April."

Silence budded between them, stretching wide and dizzying Micah. And then Shae scowled at him. "How could you be such a shithead?"

"Princess, don't cuss," he scolded automatically. When was the last time he'd had to do that? He knew right away— before Laurel had swept into their lives with her positive attitude, healthy meals, and proper manners.

A shithead. Dammit, Shae was spot on. He *was* a shithead. And an asshole. And now he was punishing his daughter for it too?

He was the failure. Not Laurel.

"Daddy, I want her to come back. I love her."

It was in that moment, staring into his daughter's tearful eyes, that he knew he did too.

He kissed his daughter on the head, told her to go back to sleep, then plopped down at the kitchen table with a beer, his phone twirling in his hand.

He needed to say sorry to Laurel. Needed to get her the remainder of the money he owed her. And most of all, he needed to stop fucking stalling.

Quickly, he dialed her number and waited, not knowing exactly what he was going to say, but knowing hearing her voice was going to both break him and put him back together again. The phone rang and rang and rang, and his heart sank and sank and sank, and then Laurel's recorded voice blared into his ear about leaving a message.

He hung up before the *beep* and immediately dialed his sister. Only two rings, but it was enough time for the dark thoughts to infiltrate his mind. Laurel had left his apartment a few hours ago—when night still coated the sky. What if something happened to her? What if Russo had been watching and took her—payback for things going awry with the last assignment? Would he ever be able to forgive himself if she received so much as a fucking scratch on her body?

April answered the phone, and Micah demanded, "Where is she?"

"Whoa, what are you yelling at me for, brother?"

"Goddammit, April. Is she there with you or not?"

One second passed. Then two. At three, Micah's heart suddenly felt like it was going to burst into millions of microscopic pieces. "Yeah," she eventually said, low, as if she was trying to keep quiet.

Micah closed his eyes and released a breath. *Thank god.* "Let me talk to her."

"Micah, do you really think that after you told her off and demanded she get out of your life—and more importantly Shae's life, the little girl she fell head over heels for—she wants anything to do with you?"

Hearing his sister's voice instead of Laurel's was straining him to the limit. "Just let me talk to her," he snapped.

"She called you an asshole," April spouted into the phone. "And the meanest man she's ever met. And if you know anything about my best friend, it's that she hardly ever cusses, so that right there is your answer as to exactly why I can't let you talk to her."

"I never meant what I said to her, though. She has to understand that." He scraped his fingernail down the paper label of the bottle, ripping a jagged line through it. "And she has to know that I'm sorry."

April let out a high-pitched whistle. "And how does that feel, lying to yourself like that?"

Lying? "What are you talking about?"

"Are you forgetting who you're talking to, big brother? The girl who grew up in the same cockroach-infested house as you did?"

He rubbed the back of his neck, cringing against the image that brought about. "What does that have to do with you accusing me of lying?"

She sighed loudly, and by the tone in her voice, he could imagine her ticking off the reasons on her fingers. "One, you're not the only one who had a drunk for a father who cared about his daily intake of alcohol more than his own children. Two, you're not the only one who hated every ounce of every minute that he was around us. And three, you're not the only one who realized at a very young age that we had zero chance at love because we'd never witnessed it ourselves. So, yes, I think when you say you didn't mean anything you said to Laurel, you're full of shit. Piles of it. You pushed away my best friend for the very reason you've pushed away every other woman who has come into your life."

With every one of his sister's words, Micah's chest constricted tighter and tighter. His legs grew restless, and he shot out of his chair. "You don't know what you're talking about." He'd never once thought about his chance at love.

"Really?" April asked, not sounding at all like she was asking for an actual answer. "Not counting Shae, when's the last time you told a girl you loved her?"

Never. He'd never said that to a woman—not even Shae's mom. They'd dated in college, but that was all it had been.

Silence filled the line. Filled the kitchen. He leaned his elbows on the counter and ran a hand over his face as April's voice filled his ear. "That's what I thought."

Was April right? Had he pushed Laurel away because he was scared of falling in love, because he'd never had that type of role model?

He let the idea drift through his thoughts, down and up and into every part of his body, feeling the weight of it, and one thing became very clear as he let that thought finally settle in his chest, right above his heart. He wasn't scared of *falling* in love.

He was scared of *failing* at love.

And maybe it was time to fix that.

Chapter Sixteen

Laurel leaned her head back on the couch and closed her tear-soaked eyes. If she held her breath, she could hear it: the low echo of his voice—Micah's voice. God it hurt, thinking his name. Because then that name would materialize into the image of his eyes, his face, the rare smile he slipped her when he wasn't consumed with the darkness around him. Or the brightness in his eyes when he looked at his daughter.

The three of them could've been so good together.

Could've been. Those words hurt too.

With the phone pinched between her shoulder and ear, April told her brother good-bye. And though it made Laurel's chest feel like it was being cracked and ripped and shredded apart, Laurel knew she had to say good-bye to him too. For good.

The couch dipped and April patted her leg. "Well, I have good news and bad news."

Laurel wiped her eyes and rolled her head to the side. "Can I just have the good?"

"He loves you." April's nose scrunched up, sending crinkles out toward the edges of her face. "And I'm not going to start in on how weird that is — my brother falling in love with my best friend. Because it is, mega weird."

He loved her, he loved her, he loved her. Okay, *ouch*, that hurt way too much. Laurel covered her face with her hands, fighting off the stinging in the corners of her eyes. "Bad. I need the bad too."

April laughed. "At least I know the feelings are mutual." Laurel wasn't looking at her best friend, but she could tell by the long inhale of breath, what was coming next was going to be painful. "The bad news," April continued, "is he doesn't know what to do with the feelings he has for you. They scare him to death, and it might take him a while to figure it out."

Laurel nodded, giving herself a moment to organize those words and then the thought that Micah wasn't going to be sorting out anything. He'd told her what he really felt. Things were done, and she needed to move past it.

She shrank into the couch and cringed as she said to April, "I'll start looking for apartments tomorrow."

Her best friend smiled gently. "You can stay here as long as you need."

Eight days. It had taken Micah eight days and almost two hundred miles to track down the one person he knew could help him. The only person he knew who had gotten out from under the mob's hand. His father.

Inside, it felt like all his organs had thrown up on each other. An acidic burning eating at his bones as he stomped over trash and debris, deeper and deeper into the alley. Leave it to his father to request to meet beside a goddamn Dumpster in Jersey City.

Cool air washed over his neck and arms, the sound of his boot soles crunching echoed into the night. The alley was empty, but that didn't mean Micah would let his guard down. He shook his head to himself. It happened once, and he'd make damn sure it never happened again.

"Son," a scraggly voice called out. Micah's entire body seized. Behind the metal Dumpster, leaning against a door labeled The Drunken Bird, his father smiled.

A bar. *Looks like things never change.*

"Hate to break it to you," Micah said, coming to a stop near a large pile of trash bags. He clenched his teeth against the sour stench. "But I stopped being your son the day you left me to take care of my sister alone."

"Nice to see you too, Micah." The man chuckled, his yellowed, glossy eyes glinting in the dim glow from the light above the door. It was a weird feeling, staring at the man he used to look up to when he was a kid. Like a splinter in his finger he couldn't find. It stung, but then it didn't. Long hair hung over the spread of wrinkles around the man's eyes and down along the sides of his thin lips. Weird, too, that even after a decade those eyes hadn't lost their potency. It wasn't a surprise that his father had been a successful enforcer. Those eyes would be pretty convincing to someone who didn't know him.

"I see," the man added, "that even with my absence, you inherited my smart mouth." His head cocked to the side. "How is she? Your sister?"

"Doing much better than you." Micah glared at him, at the holes in his jeans and the tattered tips of his shoes. "But if you want to know more than that, you can call her yourself." He eased a step forward, the itch to cut to the chase prickling at his heels. "You said you could help me."

His father's arms dropped to his sides, hands splayed along the bar door. "You know…I wish I didn't have to." Micah rolled his eyes. *Yeah, well, I wish I didn't have to be standing in an alley with the man who used to think extracurricular activities for a six- and four-year-old involved playing pool in a bar.* His father continued, "I wish I could have raised you better. The both of you. That you could've grown up in the suburbs somewhere, lived in a nice house."

Ouch, that stung. Because it was exactly what he wanted for Shae. And Laurel. And he wasn't sure he was going to be able to pull it off. Especially with his father trying to take a trip down memory lane instead of telling him how to get out.

"How'd you do it? Leave without repercussions?" Micah prompted.

His father shook his head. "You don't want to do it the way I did. By leaving everything and everyone. At the time I thought it was the only way, but now I know there are other ways."

For fifteen minutes, Micah stood and listened to this man explain that the first step Micah needed to take was to remove himself from any criminal activity and commit himself to a new lifestyle that was free of crime. He needed to change the group of people he associated with; making new friends was essential to getting out of organized crime.

Micah hadn't ever been arrested or charged for involvement in organized crime, so there was no need to hire a defense attorney or cooperate with the police. He was to move out of the city, get a decent job, and slowly cut his ties with any associates he'd had contact with.

He left the alley with a "thanks" to the man, and his mind racing.

Chapter Seventeen

Laurel sidestepped a spinning six-year-old just in time that his extended "wings" didn't knock the mound of base-ten blocks from her grip. Kids filled the hallways, their carefree voices echoing alongside the classroom buildings.

"Miss Harris, I got a pet lizard yesterday!" Lilly, one of her high-spirited students, shouted from the grass. "His name is Lizardy."

Laurel laughed. "Clever name. Maybe you could bring him to share on Friday?"

Lilly's eyes twinkled, a wide smile across her face. Would she ever get used to this? The way a few simple words could brighten a child's day?

Automatically, her mind drifted to Shae, wondering what she would want to bring to class to share, and the heaviness returned. Three months to the day had passed since she had left them. Micah and Shae and their tiny apartment. And not a day had passed that she hadn't thought about them. Wished she could see them again.

She was happy here, teaching at the elementary school her parents had taught at when she was growing up. Sort of. Mainly, she just wished she could know how they were doing. If Micah was still coming home battered and bruised. How Shae was adjusting to first grade. If they were back to eating their meals at the bar or if Shae was teaching her dad how to make simple meals.

"You look like your dog died," a familiar voice broke into her thoughts. Marcy. Her mentor teacher and new friend. Together they made up the third-grade team at the tiny school. And she couldn't have asked for a sweeter advisor. She pointed to the blocks in Laurel's arms. "Is that because you're afraid teaching place value with blocks is going to turn into a cluster-you-know-what of playtime?"

Laurel laughed and shifted her load to free her lanyard of keys. Marcy took the keys from her and opened her classroom door. "Thanks. I was actually excited to teach with something other than paper and pencil."

"You might be the only teacher on the planet who enjoys the chaos of Common Core." Marcy's extra-full lips broke into a smile, her dark hair falling over her shoulder. "So what gives?" She glanced at her watch. "You have exactly thirty seconds until the bell rings to explain."

Laurel shook her head. No, she wouldn't dwell on that part of her life. She had fallen hard for Micah. Even Shae. But obviously another plan had been in store for her. Micah hadn't felt the same way, had sent her packing, and darn it, she wasn't going to get misty-eyed over this again. Especially right before the kids returned; they noticed everything.

The shrill of the bell snapped her from the thought. "We'll talk at lunch," she told her friend just as her students started filing into the room.

"We get to play with blocks!" a few boys erupted as they skipped to their seats. Others hooted their excitement.

"Okay, quiet down, class." Laurel lowered her voice—a technique she had learned from Marcy. *If you're quiet when you speak, they have to be quiet to hear you.* "Yes, we get to play with blocks but not to build towers." A collection of groans filled the room. Laurel smiled. "These are base-ten blocks, and we will be building numbers with them to help us learn place val—"

Suddenly, her classroom door swung open and a very large, very familiar figure stepped in.

Micah.

That sputter in her chest… Was that her heart stopping? What in the world was he doing here? He paused for a moment, taking in the room—the kids, the blocks, and then her. Their eyes met, and that well-remembered wave of heat that only came with *him* crept over her. Slowly, he paced toward her, letting the door close behind him.

A black T-shirt stretched across his chest and wrapped his arms, the dark color a delicious complement to his chocolate-brown hair and eyes. She remembered the reaction she'd had the first time seeing him at The Alibi, spilling her Shirley Temple all over April's shirt. If she'd been holding a drink in the classroom, surely it would've been soaking the front of her navy blouse. Every cell in her body tingled with just the sight of him, with how his intense eyes refused to look away from her.

"Laurel," he said in a steady, low-pitched voice as he

approached, his face etched with something hard like determination. *What is he up to?*

Moving into her personal space and standing only a foot in front of her, he dropped to his knees. And before she could get a word out, he took her hands in his.

"Heartbroken," he said firmly. "That's my one word."

Silence pressed between them, her skin on fire where he was touching her. Words clogged at the base of her throat. She swallowed. "Not in front of the kids."

He thrust his shoulders back, didn't smile, and pressed on. "I pushed you away because I was afraid to allow myself to love...because I didn't think I was capable of loving. Not someone like you, who I knew deserved a better life than what I could give."

She frowned, the pain of losing him and Shae rushing in—wild and unbreakable like a tidal wave. "Then why are you here now? Interrupting my math lesson?"

"Before you came into my life, I thought I knew who I was. Thought I could give Shae everything I didn't have on my own—a good school, a decent place to live...but what I didn't realize we both needed most was someone who could teach me that the right way to live isn't to live in the past. Or in fear." His fingers entwined with hers. "I'm not afraid anymore, Laurel. My past is a long story that involves my father and his preference for booze instead of his children— but it's one I promise to share with you. And it's one that will never be a part of my future, as long as you're with me."

Laurel opened her mouth to say...well, she didn't even know. She couldn't believe Micah was here, in her classroom, talking about him and her and futures. He pressed a gentle finger over her lips.

"These last three months have made me realize that I'm not the same person without you. Because you make me want to be better. For Shae…for myself…for the woman I'm in love with."

Love. Her mind didn't trip over the word at all.

Not.

One.

Bit.

But… "Micah, I can't live the life you're living." She lowered her voice to a whisper. "The fighting… I can't handle that."

"Baby, I've left that life. All of it. Sold my share of The Alibi to Ryan, bought a house here in the suburbs, enrolled Shae in a great school…" A grin pulled at the corners of his mouth. "I hear they have incredible teachers here. She starts on Monday."

"We're getting a new student!" one of her boys shouted and the class stirred, their eyes glued to the gargantuan man kneeled at her feet. *Ha! So I'm not the only one who he has that effect on.*

"Listen," Micah continued, running his thumb across her knuckles. "I've been an unforgiving asshole." At his last word, the entire class, including Laurel, gasped.

Micah's eyes widened. "Shit, that's a bad word." He faced the class, pointing at them. "Don't you ever say that, kids." Eyes back on Laurel, he stood and took her face in his hands. She couldn't help it. She melted with just that simple touch, the warmth and soft caress of his palms. "You were right all along— I wasn't parenting Shae the right way. You made me realize that. You also made me realize that I want a life with you. I want you to be the mother to Shae… To my future babies too."

"Ewww!" the class burst out in unison. Then a chorus

of questions erupted. "Are you getting married? How are babies made?"

Oh my... Laurel laughed nervously. "This is probably not the right place to talk about this."

"I vaguely recall you saying a declaration of love in front of a whole crowd was romantic."

The movie theater...the prince and princess... *He actually remembers that?*

"This," he continued, gesturing to her students, "is the crowd I'm declaring my love in front of."

A grin started to pull at the corners of her mouth. If there was something she'd never thought she'd hear, it was that. And then Micah started to tug her toward the door. "But if you'd rather be alone..." He let those words trail off and turned to the class. "Kids, can you excuse us for a second?"

The class let out a cheer, and Laurel gasped. "Micah, I can't leave them! I could be fired."

"Good thing I cleared this with the principal beforehand then, right?" The principal...but he hated school and principals and probably teachers too after the taxing childhood he'd had. Her heart warmed. He'd gone through all this trouble just to talk to her? When he could have easily waited until after school?

Just as they reached the door, it swung wide and Kathy, the school's secretary, popped her head in. She grinned wickedly, like she was up to something. "Someone need a babysitter for a few minutes?"

"Hey!" a few kids bellowed. "We're third graders, not babies!"

"Ms. Kathy, how are babies made?"

Kathy looked to Laurel and shook her head, still smiling. "I don't want to know, do I?"

"It's not what it looks like," Laurel responded quickly. Her secretary was teasing her; she could tell by the glint of humor in her gray-blue eyes. But still...could she get in trouble for this?

Kathy pointed to the door. "Go. Looks like your boyfriend has something he wants to say to you."

Boyfriend? Laurel shook her head. "He's not—"

A strong hand tightened around hers and pulled her out the door. Cool fall air blasted against her flushed face as Micah tugged her down the hallway, her heels click-clacking along the cement. Swiftly, he opened the door to the janitor's closet, swept her in, and shut the door.

Blackness engulfed her, but she felt his hands grip her hips. His forehead tipped against hers. "Please say you will be—my girlfriend. And more. I love you, Laurel Harris, and these last few months have been agony for me. But I've realized one thing... You make my life better. In every way possible."

His life... He said he left the bar, but what about... "Are you still working the other job?" Her heart stuttered. She knew she'd never be able to consider what he was proposing if he was.

Against her forehead, she could feel him shake his head. "I cut my ties with them when I moved out here. They didn't like it, but they also didn't like the distance. I haven't been contacted in over two months."

Relief flooded her veins, and she sagged against him. Could she do this? Accept him back into her life? Her body sang in the presence of his. So alive. So, so...

She needed this man. The last few months had proved that— That even with the job of her dreams, her life still hadn't felt complete. But now? In his arms surrounded by the Micah scent she loved so much?

"Forgiveness," she whispered, swallowing in an attempt to keep her emotions in check as the heat of her word filled the small space between them. Slowly, his hands started to slide up her back, tightening into a glorious hold. "That's my one word."

He stepped closer, his chest pressing against hers, and she tipped her head back, knowing exactly where his mouth would be. Only milliseconds passed until he first kissed her cheek then his gentle lips found hers.

His tongue swept in, tentatively at first, lingering against hers in long, sweeping strokes. Delicious. The rhythm picked up, along with the beat of her heart, and needing to be closer to him—to rid the space between them—she snaked her arms around his neck and tugged her body into his.

Kissing him, feeling his hands on her, only intensified the ache in her chest. There was no question about it— This was where she belonged. In his arms. In his life.

The heat of their kiss sank down into her belly, igniting the deep longing she'd been suppressing for months. Janitor closet or not, she wanted this man, and she wanted him now.

Please don't make me beg this time!

"I couldn't help but notice," he said, his lips still against hers, "you seemed rather tongue tied back there when your students asked how babies were made." Fingers slipped under the hem of her blouse and traced a hot line around her sides, across her belly, and snapped at the elastic waistband of her flowy skirt. "Do you need a little lesson, Miss Harris?"

Laurel giggled, running her fingers into his hair. "I'm a little distracted right now. I might require a few. You know… so I *fully* comprehend."

With a smoothness only he possessed, he hitched up her skirt, smiling against her neck. "As you wish."

Epilogue

Shae saluted the judges, and just before she stepped up to the uneven bars, Micah shouted, "You've got this, Shae!" To his right, the woman in the salmon pink sweater gave him a side-eye. What? He couldn't cheer on his daughter in her first ever gymnastics competition? Then he noticed the woman eyeing his tattoos, skimming his body all the way down to his black boots with a wary pinch to her expression.

He rolled his eyes. *Whatever.* He'd never look like he belonged in suburbia, but there was something to be said for not having to throw out drunk patrons or look over his shoulder every five seconds.

In front of him, Laurel waddled toward him, her eight-month-pregnant belly sticking out in front of her, the single diamond ring catching the light of the sun. He'd endure side-eyes every minute of the day to keep this life the two of them had built together just for her.

She shifted, the variety of sodas and foil-wrapped hot

dogs almost spilling.

Hurriedly, Micah stormed down from his seat in the bleachers, scattering a few more of the skittish parents sitting nearby, and removed the sodas from her hands. "I thought you said you were going to the bathroom?"

She smiled shyly, fully aware of the audience of wary parents watching them. "I did, but then I got thirsty and the hot dogs looked so good and—"

Pressing his lips to hers, he silenced her with a kiss. "Jesus, you're adorable." She blinked up at him, surprise in her round eyes. He could stare at her all day. "And I will never get tired of the way you look at me when I do that."

A weak scowl scrunched her face, but the pink that crept into her cheeks gave her embarrassment away. "If my whacky pregnant brain recalls correctly, that's how this happened," she said, pointing her eyes in the direction of her belly.

He reached for the hot dogs too. "Which one is mine?"

Quickly, she plucked both hot dogs out of his hand. "Neither," she said and tried to rush up the bleacher steps with the slowest waddle ever. Laughing, Micah shook his head and followed. It may not have been the life he thought he'd have, but damn it all if this wasn't the life he wanted.

Acknowledgments

First and foremost I want to thank you, the reader. Your love for romance made this series exist. If you enjoyed reading this book, you can help other readers find it by RECOMMENDING it to friends and family, reading and discussion groups, online forums, or the like. You can also REVIEW it on the site where you purchased it. If you do happen to write a review, please inform me via an email to brooklynskye1@gmail.com and I'll thank you with a personal email.

I also owe thanks to everyone at Entangled who participated in the makings of this book, inside and out: Heather Howland, Stacy Cantor Abrams, Curtis Svehlak, and Katie Clapsadl.

And my family and friends. Each of you have supported me and encouraged me, and I would have never gotten to where I am without it. Thank you.

About the Author

Brooklyn Skye grew up in a small town where she quickly realized writing was an escape from small-town life. Really, she's just your average awkward girl who's obsessed with words. She writes young adult, new adult, and romance fiction. You can follow her on Twitter as @brooklyn__skye, Instagram as @brooklynskyewrites, or visit her website for updates, teasers, giveaways, and more. www.brooklyn-skye.com.

Also by Brooklyn Skye...

JUST ONE REASON

FRAGILE LINE